STEALING HOME

MARY STOLZ

STEALING HOME

A Scholastic edition

HarperTrophy
A Division of HarperCollins*Publishers*

Library of Congress Cataloging-in-Publication Data
Stolz, Mary, date
    Stealing Home/ by Mary Stolz.
        p.   cm.
    Summary: Though they still listen to baseball and go fishing, Thomas
and his grandfather find life in their small house in Florida changed when
Great-aunt Lizzy comes to stay.
    ISBN 0-06-021154-7. — ISBN 0-06-021157-1 (lib. bdg.)
    ISBN 0-06-440528-1 (pbk.)
    [1. Grandfathers—Fiction.   2. Great-aunts—Fiction.   3. Afro-
Americans—Fiction.   4. Old age—Fiction.   5. Florida—Fiction.
6. Baseball—Fiction]   I. Title.
PZ7.S87585Sr   1992   92-5226
[E]—dc20   CIP
                                                                  AC

This is for Johanna,
with love from Vóvó Molly

Thomas, standing beside his grandfather's chair, shivered and put his hands in his armpits.

"People think it's always warm in Florida, don't they, Grandfather?"

"People who don't live here might."

"It sure isn't warm this morning."

"February!" Grandfather waved his hand. "A most unstable month. Would you like a fire?"

"That's a *good* idea."

Getting up, Grandfather opened the door of the cast-iron stove that stood on flagstones in a corner of their living room. With kindling and

1

a couple of small logs from a brass bucket beside the stove, he soon had a merry blaze going.

"Better?" he asked.

"Yes," said Thomas, a bit crankily.

"Should've made one earlier, perhaps. Only I didn't think to."

"That's all right," said Thomas, relenting.

Grandfather was skinny and pretty old, but he never seemed to mind what the weather was like and never complained about it. He didn't say he wished it would get warmer, or cooler, or that the rain would go away, or the rain would come, the way most people did.

Now he didn't say he wished the fog would lift, though here it was—cold, gray, so thick that Thomas, still shivering a little, couldn't see through the window. Even Ringo, Thomas's cat, who usually wanted to stay outdoors in the morning, had sprinted back to the house after just a brief visit to the garden, where his duck, Ivan the Terrible, had come rushing out of the mist to greet him.

Ringo had greeted Ivan with a lick on the

head, then left him outside, where he was still quacking and calling.

"Poor terrible Ivan," Thomas said. "He's lonely. Do you suppose we should let him in for a little bit?"

"Absolutely not!" said Grandfather. "I have explained, more than once, that a duck is not a cat. There is no known way to house-train a duck."

Thomas shrugged. Ivan would make out okay in the yard, in the fog, and he didn't really want to let him in the house. Actually, he didn't want Ivan, period. But there was no way to get rid of him.

He had come into their lives last spring, when Ringo had appeared one morning trailed by a tottery duckling.

"Lookit, Grandfather!" Thomas had shouted. "A little duck followed Ringo home! From the beach, I guess! Come see! Hurry!"

Grandfather, weeding in his stir-fry garden, straightened and walked over, carrying some collard greens. Pinching the tip of his nose, which he did when he was thinking, he studied a very small duckling covered with fluffy brown-and-yellow down. It kept toppling onto its bill, till it finally squatted in the grass, eyes fixed on Ringo. One of its wings looked odd to Thomas.

Ringo, looming over the duck, complained to Thomas. *"Mewow!"* he said. "This duck here followed me home! What am I going to do?" he cried, and twined around Thomas's leg.

"Well, well," said Grandfather. "We seem to have here a genuine case of imprinting."

"Huh?" said Thomas.

"I believe this is how it happened—" Grandfather began, and Thomas, who felt that his grandfather knew how just about everything happened, listened alertly.

"No doubt the mother of this fellow—*if* it's a fellow; we can't be sure of that yet—hatched her clutch down on the beach, and this one didn't get out of the shell on time. She assumed the egg was a dud and led the rest of her brood away to a freshwater pond."

"That wasn't so nice of her."

"Natural, Thomas, quite natural. She

couldn't take chances with the rest of her family, waiting for an egg that might never hatch."

"So then what happened?"

"I'd say that after she left, this critter managed to peck its way into the world. And just then—along came Ringo! There are creatures—for some reason especially ducks—that will take the first moving object they see for a parent. It's called 'imprinting.' The image they first see gets imprinted on their minds as the only one in the world to be followed. A newly hatched duckling will tag after a mechanical toy, if that's all it finds to attach itself to. Your duck here thinks Ringo is its mother. Father, I suppose. So it followed him home to us."

Thomas frowned. "That's sort of sad, isn't it?" When Grandfather said nothing, he asked, "What's wrong with its wing? It looks funny."

Grandfather hunkered down, put his vegetables to one side, and gently touched the maimed wing. "Hmmm. I think I know what happened."

Thomas smiled and waited. His grandfather didn't just give information. He told a story.

"Some little while ago, Thomas, a ghost crab was coming up through one of her many tunnels on the beach to scout for a bite of breakfast. She reached the entrance just as your duck here—or Ringo's duck, let's say—flopped out of the shell. Then—well *then*, alas and sad to say, she simply nipped off the tip of this wing. You can see how she got it, right to the first joint. I would say that Ringo appeared at that very moment. The crab ran back to safety, the duck looked at the cat, and *'Lo! and be whole!'* as Krazy Kat used to say, imprinting occurred. I wonder what would have happened if the crab had appeared in time to be the first moving object to meet this duck's eyes?"

"Well, he wouldn't have followed a ghost crab down a tunnel, would he? Especially not one that had just bit off part of his wing."

"Still, it's curious to think about. A fowl imprinted on a crab. Probably would've been a first for Mother Nature."

"Does his wing hurt awfully bad?" Thomas asked, screwing up his face till his nose wrinkled and his eyes were almost closed. He always made faces at the thought of pain. Mostly his own, of course, but here was this poor little wounded duck right in front of him.

"I don't think so. And animals can take a deal of pain without complaint. It'll heal. But that joint is where his primary feathers would have grown. Without them, he won't be able to fly, and *that* is going to be a problem. For him and us."

"Can't we keep him? He's awfully cute. I can make a cage to keep—"

"No cage," said Grandfather.

"But he'll fly away!"

"Thomas. You must listen better. I just explained that flying is going to be out of the question. Besides, you can bet he'll stick to Ringo like a burr." Grandfather stroked his beard. "Let us hope Ringo continues to feel fatherly."

"You mean he might kill it? Ringo wouldn't do that, Grandfather. He's going to adopt it, you'll see."

7

"Possibly," said Grandfather, lifting one brow, a trick he had that Thomas couldn't get the hang of.

That had been months ago. At first they had just called the duck, "Duck." In time, when Ringo's pretty little duckling grew up to become an ugly large drake, Grandfather named him Ivan the Terrible. "It is our poor luck," he said, "to be stuck with a Muscovy duck."

"He sure is awful looking, Grandfather."

"And has a disposition like broken glass. Ringo still seems to like him. Or tolerate him. But then, animals don't care what other creatures look like. One of the many ways in which they prove themselves superior to human beings."

Ivan was big, with black-and-white plumage. He had a bill like a dug-up bone and a huge red bump of lumpy naked skin on his forehead. He tried to attack strangers, and now and then made a run at Grandfather or Thomas. He was messy and greedy, and Grandfather had been obliged to fence the vegetable garden against him.

All in all, Ivan was a problem that they didn't know how to get rid of. He couldn't fly away. He wouldn't run away. And Grandfather and Thomas couldn't bring themselves to have him put away.

"He's an awful duck," Thomas's friend Donny Price said when he had to fend Ivan's bite off with his foot, which happened pretty often. "How can you stand having him live with you?"

To which Thomas always replied, "He's gotta live somewhere, doesn't he?"

So here, on this cold morning, were Grandfather, Thomas, and Ringo, sitting close to the stove, while Ivan the Terrible squawked alone in the fog.

"It's cozy, isn't it?" Thomas said. "I like just the three of us being cozy like this." Cozy was one of Thomas's favorite words.

Grandfather pinched the end of his nose, looked around the room, looked at his hands. "Thomas, about that—"

"About what?" Thomas prodded when

Grandfather fell silent.

"About the three of us being together. There's something I have to tell you."

"Oh?" Thomas said warily. "What?"

"We are going to have a visitor."

"Mr. McCallam?" Thomas brightened. "That's good."

Grandfather's friend, Mr. Milo McCallam, who owned a small motel in a town near Miami, drove over for a fishing weekend two or three times a year. Sometimes they fished from an old pier that jutted into the Gulf of Mexico; sometimes Mr. McCallam wore his waders and cast from the surf. At least once during a visit they'd go out on the bay in Grandfather's old wooden boat, with its five-horsepower motor, a pail for bailing, and a paddle for emergency use.

"No, Thomas, not Mr. McCallam this time. My sister-in-law, Linzy, is coming to pay us a visit." Still not looking at Thomas, Grandfather added, "It sounds to me as if she's planning on a pretty long one."

"Oh," said Thomas, not so brightly now.

10

He and his grandfather and Ringo lived in this house by the Gulf of Mexico. This *small* house. Just big enough for the three of them. It had been that way for all of Thomas's life that he could remember, and was how he wanted it to be for all the rest of it.

"A pretty long visit, huh? She says that?" he asked now.

"I'm afraid—I mean, yes. I think that's the way of it."

"Grandfather?"

"Yes, Thomas?"

"I'll have to sleep in the living room, won't I?"

"Yes."

Thomas thought for a moment and then said, "Is she my grandmother?"

"Thomas! My wife was your grandmother. You surely know that."

"I guess. I mean, yes. But I didn't know her."

"No," Grandfather said. For a while he looked down again at his big hands, not speaking. His wife, Thomas's grandmother, had died years before Thomas was born. There was a picture of her on Grandfather's chest of

11

drawers. A pretty lady. In the picture she was way younger than Grandfather. Thomas's mother had been their only child.

In Thomas's room, on his dresser, was a picture in a double frame of his parents. Weeks passed when he didn't even see it. Then a day would come when he'd take it down and look at them, his own young mother and father, for a long time. They had died together in an automobile accident when he'd been only a year old. He didn't like to think about that, and usually did not, but sometimes they got into his dreams. All that long time ago, he had come to live here, with his grandfather.

Thomas guessed that he was imprinted on Grandfather.

"My sister-in-law, Linzy," Grandfather went on, "is your grandmother's sister. That makes her your great-aunt. I guess you can just call her Aunt Linzy."

"I suppose," Thomas said gloomily. "How long is she going to stay?"

Grandfather drew a deep breath, slowly let it out. "I don't know," he said at last.

"Why is she coming? She never did before. Or maybe when I was too little to remember?"

"My sister-in-law hasn't left Chicago in over forty years."

"Chicago?" Thomas exclaimed. "Oh, boy, I bet she gets to see the Cubs all the *time*."

"I doubt if she sees them any of the time."

"Doesn't like baseball, huh?"

"Not when I last knew her. Of course, that was a long time ago."

"Do you suppose she'll want to fish with us?"

"I shouldn't think so."

"What *does* she like to do?"

"Bat cleanup."

Thomas looked at his grandfather suspiciously. "She's an old lady, isn't she?"

"Yes, Thomas. I was trying to be funny—"

Thomas got it. "Bat cleanup! About somebody who doesn't even go to games! That's *neat*, Grandfather—that's funny as heck."

"All right, Thomas. I am sufficiently gratified. What I meant is that as I recall, Linzy tidies up after people. Sees that things are neat and clean. All around. All the time. She lived with your grandmother and me for nearly a year when we were first married. I think she scrubbed the soles of our shoes when we weren't looking."

Thomas gazed around the living room. "Oh, boy," he said. "I hope she doesn't want to bat cleanup here."

There were lots of shelves crowded with books and their shell collection and pieces of driftwood and petrified wood and smooth bottle glass that they had found over the years—except that you couldn't find bottle glass anymore since practically everything was plastic—and nice sculptures that Grandfather carved from beach stones and driftwood. There was a fossil of a fish an inch long and fifty million years old. Grandfather had found it in North Carolina when he was a boy.

They had two games tables. On one they kept a jigsaw puzzle going. They got most of these from the library but owned a few, including three they couldn't finish, or even get well started on, though they'd tried. One was all different shades of blue. One had nothing but colored dots and the third colored swirls. Grandfather and Thomas liked puzzles with pictures on them, and when they finished one, they started another. On the other, larger table were dominoes, a checkerboard, a Scrabble set, and a couple of decks of cards. After Thomas had outgrown Go Fish, they'd taken to playing casino. But their handsomest game was the cribbage set. Grandfather had made the board himself, out of a bole of wood that he had polished till it gleamed like brown silk. He'd carved the pegs and driven one hundred twenty small holes for the streets.

Evenings, before Thomas's bedtime, they'd choose which game to play and push the others to one side. Cribbage and Scrabble were their favorites. After the game, when Thomas was in bed, Grandfather would read to him for about half an hour, even though Thomas could perfectly well read to himself.

"I like it this way," Thomas would say. "It's cozy."

Grandfather's desk was heaped with letters, maps, bills, postcards, snapshots, a stapler, a calendar from last year, gardening information bulletins from the Florida Cooperative Extension Service, newspaper clippings, a mug full of ballpoint pens—only a few of which worked—Grandfather's pipes, a collegiate dictionary, some old score cards of Pirates games, a bowl containing elastic bands, paper clips, some screws, several picture hooks with the nails missing, a few pennies . . .

There was also Thomas's marble. He had only the one, as nobody at his school played marbles. It was a taw, a shooter streaked brown and white and orange, and pretty scuffed up. A marble that had been, in its time, played with a lot. Its time had been Thomas's father's time, and the taw had belonged to him.

Now it belonged to Thomas, who valued but never played with it.

He gave up on the desk.

His ball and bat and fielder's glove were in a corner where he'd left them a couple of days ago. Grandfather had dropped the morning paper—all scrambled up—on the floor beside his chair. There was sand everywhere, tracked in from the beach, that they hadn't got around to sweeping up, and Thomas noticed for the first time that the furniture was maybe a bit dusty.

"She wouldn't want to clean up just on a visit, would she, do you think?"

"I hope not. Actually, I don't know her very well. We didn't get along together, that year she lived with us. We bickered a lot. She was as different as could be from Marta."

Grandfather, who liked to tell tales of olden times as much as Thomas liked listening to them, hardly ever spoke of Marta, his lost young wife. Thomas didn't ask about her, in case it would make Grandfather sad. He didn't ask about his own parents in case it would make himself sad.

"Grandfather. If you didn't get along together, and bickered and all that, why is she coming to visit us?"

"She simply wrote out of the blue and said she was. Not a by-your-leave or anything."

"But then why do we—why should we—"

17

"She's family. Your grandmother's sister. You want me to write and say, 'Get lost, Linzy, old girl, we don't want you here'?"

"No. You can't do that. Did you tell her I have to give up my room?"

"I did. I tried to put it tactfully. I explained that we have but two bedrooms, that our house is very small. She said that she won't mind being crowded."

"Oh. Oh, well . . . if that's what she said."

Again he looked around the room. Should they maybe beat her to it? Tidy up before she came?

"So when's she getting here?"

"That part isn't clear. She needs time to wind things up in Chicago first, is what she says."

"Oh." Thomas made a face. "Wind things up? Grandfather—does that mean she's going to move *in* with us? I mean, not just *visit?*"

"Of course not! She'll just—ah—stay for a while."

"Maybe she'll change her mind and not come."

"I don't think so," Grandfather said sharply.

"We are going to be gracious and understanding about this, Thomas. You do understand?"

"Yes, Grandfather." Thomas looked out the window. The fog seemed to be lessening. "If it clears up, we could go fishing."

"Have you finished your homework?"

"Yup."

"Let's get the gear together."

As they assembled their fishing equipment, Thomas said, "Anyway, Grandfather, it's almost the end of February!"

Grandfather smiled. "So it is, Thomas."

"So *that* means the Pirates will be here for spring training pretty soon."

"March fourth," Grandfather said cheerfully.

"You got tickets?"

"Four home games. Astros, Cardinals, White Sox, and the Cardinals again."

Thomas sighed happily. Fishing today, and pretty soon the Pirates playing at McKechnie Field in Bradenton. It would be dumb to spoil things thinking about this Aunt Linzy. No matter what Grandfather said, she might change her mind about coming to Florida. Or when she saw how small their house was, *then* she'd change her mind about staying with them.

If she didn't, what then?

Well, then he'd be gracious and understanding, or Grandfather would know the reason why.

2

FEBRUARY PASSED WITH NO FURTHER word from Aunt Linzy. Occupied with daily life—school, fishing, card games, cribbage, Donny, reading, listening to Grandfather's tales of olden days, Thomas forgot about her.

Each spring, when the Pirates played at McKechnie Field, Grandfather got seats for as many games as they could afford. These were the only live ones Thomas ever saw. Since the television set had broken, they were the only games either of them saw.

"How long until we can get the TV fixed?"

Thomas asked sometimes.

Grandfather lifted his shoulders.

"In time for the World Series, maybe?"

"Maybe. Anyway, Thomas—television games are not the real thing. Baseball's a game you should be at a park for, and it should be played in the afternoon, on grass, in the sun."

"I guess," said Thomas, who would've settled for TV when spring training was over.

Now they were on their way to McKechnie to see the first game with St. Louis. They carried cushions to ease the hardness of bleacher seats, and Thomas had his fielder's glove in case he got to catch a foul ball, a moment of happiness denied him so far, but Grandfather said it was not impossible—after all, somebody had to catch them.

"I sure hope Ozzie's in the lineup today," Grandfather said. He was crazy over short-stops. Ernie Banks, who had played a long time for the Chicago Cubs, had been his hero, but after Ernie left the game, Ozzie Smith moved into the field of Grandfather's heart.

"Which one's better?" Thomas asked now. "Ernie Banks or Ozzie?"

"I couldn't choose. Ernie was inspired, dazzling. But so's Ozzie. They say Honus Wagner was the greatest shortstop who ever played, but who knows?"

"Did you see him, Grandfather?"

"You know, strange as it may seem, there actually was a time that was before my time. He was out of the game before I was born."

"Oh."

"Probably," Grandfather went on, stopping for a red light and fetching a great sigh, "probably Ozzie knows the end of his playing days is in sight. Baseball is the only sport that makes a person sad—that is, someone watching, not playing. A rookie reliever blows a save his first time out—how can you not feel for him? Rookies are so *tender*, and the old heroes so bruised and brave. Baseball makes the people who love it unhappy a lot of the time, but you tell me— whoever felt his heart wrenched because a nose tackle hangs up his spikes?"

"Maybe some peo—"

23

"How can you ache for a player whose eyes you've never seen? An aging fireballer, out on the mound with nowhere to hide, behind in the count on every batter—that *hurts*. A one-time MVP with half a dozen Gold Gloves lets an easy grounder get through his legs in the World Series . . . you *die* for him."

"I guess," said Thomas, who wasn't old enough to ache for aging heroes.

They arrived at the stadium in time for batting practice. Thomas gave Grandfather his glove to hold and headed for the clubhouse, hoping to catch a player on his way to the field and get his smudged, scarred baseball signed. He'd had it since the day two years before when Grandfather, driving past Al Lang Stadium in St. Pete, where the New York Mets trained, had seen a ball fly out of the park and roll into the street. Jamming on the brakes, he'd leaped from the truck and grabbed it from under the nose of a young man sprinting across the sidewalk in pursuit. So far, it had no signatures. Thomas was rather small, and not inclined to push. Not every player bothered to

24

sign, but some would stop to take a ball and pen from an outstretched hand and scribble their name. Of course they took the ball and pen nearest to them, and could not be expected, Grandfather had pointed out, to look around for a small boy jumping on the edge of the crowd.

"Any luck?" Grandfather asked, when Thomas met him at the hot-dog stand nearest the ramp leading to their seats.

"Grandfather! I got Bobby Bonilla! He signed my ball, and he spoke to me!"

"Well! Well, that's *wonderful*, Thomas! What did he say?"

"He said, 'There you are, son.'"

"Think of it!"

"Yes. Everybody had just about gone and only a couple of grown-ups were still hanging around and Bobby came out after all the other guys had already left for the field, and he saw us and the *first* person he took the ball from was ME! And he signed it and handed it back to me, and he said, *'There you are, son.'*" Thomas sighed and closed his eyes. "It was an Everest of joy."

That was what Grandfather called it when something wonderful happened. An Everest of joy.

"I should think so. Well. Shall we proceed?"

"Oh, sure," Thomas said dreamily, turning and turning the baseball in his hand, carefully, so as not to smudge.

"Are you too dazzled for hot dogs?"

"No!"

They bought a program to keep score on, a hot dog each, and large paper cups of Coke. Then they made their way to the bleachers and sat there happily watching the heroes of the world's greatest game swing their sticks in the batting cage.

Thomas thought that Grandfather was right. Baseball on the TV screen was not baseball in the bleachers, in the sun, in the afternoon, played on grass. Replays were fine, but didn't make up for seeing outfielders slap their gloves and go into a crouch, ready to run in, run back, ready for grounders, for fly balls, for what came their way. On TV you couldn't really see the shortstop birddog a runner on second, or men at first and third charge the plate on a bunt.

"Two different games," Grandfather would say.

Just the same, Thomas hoped they'd get the set fixed sometime before the Series.

Hours later, homeward bound, they went over the game inning by inning. They were happy that Ozzie had indeed been there, and that he'd made a couple of electrifying plays—one diving catch taking away a sure double, and one leap straight up from a standing position that Grandfather said Ringo would envy. They were also happy that Pittsburgh had won.

"I liked it, Grandfather, when you said it was a bunt situation, and that guy beside you said, *'Sez you.'*"

"It was obvious. We had a close game, man on first, pitcher at the plate. Not a good hitting pitcher. He had to try to lay one down and get the runner in scoring position."

27

The Cardinal at the plate had indeed bunted, popping up for the second out.

"Hah!" Grandfather's neighbor crowed.

Grandfather only smiled. "I didn't say he'd be successful, just it was what he had to do."

Thomas loved listening to his Grandfather's comments during a game, even when sometimes he didn't quite understand and things were moving too fast for him to ask.

"What's the butcher-boy play?" he asked now. "You said that when *Bobby*"—he paused reverently—"was up in the third."

"When a hitter fakes a bunt but takes a swing instead, that's the butcher-boy play. It deceives the pitcher until it's too late to change his delivery, and it's risky, because if the first or third baseman has sneaked in for the bunt, what's he to do if the hitter swings and connects? A good play to use now and then, but only if you connect."

"Bobby did, all right. Two for three, he went. If that dumb bunny of an ump hadn't called a third strike on him that any dope could see was a ball, he'd've been three for three! That umpire was crazy!"

"Umpires may be crazy, but they are *always* right, Thomas. Even when they aren't. Besides, aren't they entitled to make errors, just like the players?"

"You always say that."

"I always mean it."

A few miles passed in silence, and then Grandfather said tentatively, "Thomas, have you faced the fact that Bonilla will be a free agent in a couple of years?"

"So?"

"So—there's a good possibility that he'd go to another club."

"Not a chance!" Thomas said, laughing. "Bobby Bo with a different team? No way, Grandfather. No way."

Grandfather started to speak, blew out a breath, then concentrated on traffic.

When they parked at the back of the house, Ringo rose from his perch on the porch railing and Ivan came raging out of the sea oats, squawking, flapping his good wing, waving his stump.

"Whew," said Grandfather, gently pushing him away with one shoe. "This fellow gets more ornery every day."

"I'll feed them," Thomas said.

Although Ivan spent his waking hours eating seeds, insects, pebbles, bits of this and that picked up here and there, he always demanded a proper meal when Ringo got his. Sometimes he tried to snatch something from Ringo's dish, but a flick of a quick paw took care of that. Ivan apparently still considered the cat to be his parent, or his boss, and Ringo was the only creature he didn't seem to hate.

Sometimes Thomas fed them both in the yard, but today Ringo came into the house to be with them. He always did that when they'd been away for a while.

"People think cats don't care about company, don't they, Grandfather?" Thomas asked after dinner, when they were playing cribbage and Ringo was on his lap, purring as he slept.

"People who don't know them well, perhaps."

"Cats *like* to be with people."

"Ringo certainly seems to enjoy our company. Especially yours."

"I know that," Thomas said. He jumped his peg three holes and grinned triumphantly. "There, Grandfather! I skunked you!"

It had been a fine day, a triumphant day, and when Thomas went to bed, he lay for a while looking at the outline of his baseball on the windowsill.

"You know something," he said to Ringo, draped at the bottom of the blanket, "I'm not going to ask anyone else to sign it. It's going to be my Bobby Bonilla ball. I guess Bobby Bonilla is my hero, the way Ernie Banks and Ozzie Smith are Grandfather's heroes."

He looked into the half-attentive sand-colored eyes.

"Grandfather says if cats played ball, they'd all be shortstops. He says that's the fanciest, prettiest position and the best of all, and he says it takes cats like Ernie and Ozzie to play it. But let me tell you something, Ringo—it takes a *lion* to cover third. . . ."

Ringo stretched and turned on his back.

"And don't you worry," Thomas continued. "Bobby Bonilla will never leave the Pirates."

Ringo yawned.

Outside, palm-tree fronds rustled with a sound like rain, and a screech owl's fluttering call sounded close by.

Thomas yawned too, and fell asleep.

Toward the end of March, Grandfather and Thomas began work in the stir-fry garden, now fenced against Ivan. They planted seeds that would in a short time poke green tendrils out of the earth and in a couple of months yield snap beans, eggplants, peppers sweet and hot, lettuces, collards, okra, and summer squash. They drove stakes for tomato plants and planted nasturtiums all around the vegetable beds. Grandfather claimed that nasturtiums discouraged weeds and insects, and sometimes he put them on salad, as a garnish, because it looked pretty.

"Now, Thomas," he said, when all was well within the fence, "we shall see to our flowers."

Donny's mother, Mrs. Price, said Grandfather could probably make a mop handle burst into bloom, but he declined to try, for fear of disappointment all around.

In a border at the back of the house, they planted blue ageratum, white alyssum, salmon-colored geraniums; and in window boxes along the front and back porches they put petunia plants that in a little while would drip down the sides in all sorts of colors. The beds against the front of the house displayed daisies and foxgloves, begonias, snapdragons, and sweet william. These were annuals, pulled up each winter. There were oleanders and hibiscus bushes along the driveway. Under the great live oak in the front yard were lilies that opened only after rain showers. They were fragile and very pretty and were called rain lilies.

Migratory birds arrived in full mating plumage. They sang the daylong and into the evening. Establishing, said Grandfather, their territories. The air was filled with melodies, and with mockingbirds putting all these airs together in happy imitation. Thomas loved it when the springtime birds were around, loved how they sang and colored the air.

In North America, the regular baseball season began.

In Florida, the snook season opened.

Days, weeks, then months passed with Grandfather and Thomas happily occupied working in the garden, reading, cooking—Grandfather was an A-one cook—playing checkers and cribbage and cards, working jigsaw puzzles that had scenery to guide them.

They listened to National League games.

"What've you two got against the American League?" Mr. McCallam had once asked. "The game's the game, isn't it?"

"Milo—in 1945, Branch Rickey brought Jackie Robinson into the major leagues. Until then no matter how great he was, a black man played in the *Negro* Leagues. Satchel Paige,

Buck Ewing, Josh Gibson, Cool Papa Bell—they weren't ball players. They were *Negro* ball players. But Branch Rickey tapped Jackie Robinson, black as they come, and sent him up to the Montreal Royals, the Brooklyn farm team, and two years later—there was a black man at second base in Ebbetts Field, taking abuse you and I wouldn't begin to put up with and winning every award in sight. Before Mr. Rickey and Jackie Robinson, a black man didn't even *think* major league. After them—well, even you know where we've gone since. That's why I'm a National League man, always have been, always will be."

"What about you, Thomas?" Mr. McCallam said. "You just follow your granddad's lead?"

"Sure do. I like his lead."

Grandfather had given a quirkily proud smile.

"Have you and Grandfather gone after snook yet?" Donny asked as he and Thomas walked the beach looking for good shells. (His mother

36

had said he should call Grandfather "Mr. Weaver," but the first time he did, Grandfather turned all around, looking into corners, at the ceiling, at the floor, and finally said, "Who's this Weaver fellow, Donny? Some ringer from the American League you've brought in to take my spot?" and that was that.)

"Lots of times," Thomas said. He leaned over to pick up a moonshell, but it was broken.

"Have you caught any?"

"We never catch any."

"You did that one time."

"Not to keep."

"Aren't you going to still try? Isn't the snook season over pretty soon?"

"This weekend."

"So?"

"Mr. McCallam's coming tomorrow, and the three of us can go together. For a last cast, Grandfather says."

Donny looked wistful, but said no more. His family was vegetarian, and he was not allowed to fish. Vegetarianism, said Grandfather, was an honorable position to take, but he'd never been able to achieve it. Thomas hadn't noticed that he'd tried.

In the years that he'd been fishing with his grandfather, they had caught but one snook. It was the tastiest, Grandfather said, of all piscatorial treasures. Thomas himself had yet to get a taste, as their catch that time had measured under the limit of twenty-four inches, so Grandfather had had to release it.

There were people—everyone knew it—who kept fish that were under the legal length. Spearing snook was absolutely against the law, but there were people who speared them. Grandfather and Thomas knew two men who did this and always got away with it.

Grandfather and Thomas did not break the law.

Mr. McCallam arrived on the last Thursday in June. All weekend, trying for snook, they cruised near the mangroves in their dory with its five-horsepower motor, casting toward shore. In three days they had a fine catch of mangrove snapper, grunts, flounder, and speckled trout. But the "piscatorial treasure," the snook, continued to elude them.

On Sunday evening Thomas and Mr. Mc-Callam sat in the kitchen, watching as Grandfather made his famous fish gumbo with an assortment of their catch and vegetables from the garden. The gumbo was served with Grandfather's crusty bread to dip in the sauce, and followed with his walnut pie.

"I don't see how snook could taste better than this," Thomas said, and Mr. McCallam agreed. Grandfather smiled and said modestly, "It *is* a feast for kings."

Mr. McCallam had a long drive ahead, so he left after dinner, his share of the catch cleaned and bedded in ice in a cooler. His nephew Chet, who took charge of the motel when he was away, was leaving for his summer job as a ranger in Glacier Park, so they wouldn't see Mr. McCallam again until fall.

Thomas liked Mr. McCallam but was glad to sleep in his own bed, with Ringo at the foot of it or curled in the crook of his knees.

In the middle of July, a letter arrived from Chicago. Thomas, looking at the postmark, wrinkled his nose. He really had forgotten about the aunt—great-aunt—who'd said way back in February that she was coming to pay a visit. He put the letter on the kitchen table.

When Grandfather came in from the garden, he pointed and said, "That's from your— from my— from the lady in Chicago."

"Ah. I see." Grandfather wiped his hands on his overalls and sat down. Thomas stood beside him. "Better find out what she has to say."

"Maybe she's not coming after all. Maybe that's what the letter says."

Grandfather opened the envelope, read, looked Thomas in the eye. "She's arriving by train, on Friday. We are to meet her. And we are to be—"

"I know, Grandfather. Gracious and understanding."

"Good. You remembered. See that you don't forget."

"Should I empty one of my dresser drawers

for her to put her things in?"

"Thomas—that's thoughtful. Yes, indeed. I'm glad you thought of it."

"Do you think she'll stay long, Grandfather?"

"You've asked that several times already. I have answered that I don't know, because the fact is—I don't know."

"Do you suppose you'll bicker with her?"

"Why should I do that?" Grandfather snapped.

"You *said*. You told me you and her bickered all the—"

"You and *she*, Thomas, not you and her—"

"Her and I haven't even met!"

Grandfather's mouth twitched.

Friday was hot and muggy.

Leaving Ringo outdoors with Ivan, Thomas and his grandfather, in the pickup, started for the Tampa railroad depot. Grandfather drove. Thomas, fielder's glove on the seat beside him, road map on his lap, gave directions.

"Okay, Grandfather. First we go for a long

while on the Tamiami Trail."

"North or south?"

"Oh, Grandfather! North, of course."

"Good. If you're to navigate, you must be precise."

"All right. We go north on the Tamiami Trail until—" He peered at the map. "Somewhere past Palmetto, we have to go to the right. There's a fork in the road there." Thomas thought for a moment, then asked, "How many miles to Tampa?"

"That sounds very like a poem."

"What poem?"

> "How many miles to Babylon?
> Threescore and ten.
> Can I get there by candlelight?
> Yes, and back again."

"What does that mean—threescore?"

Grandfather, who did not drive fast, was edging over to the right lane so people could pass. When that was accomplished, he said, "A score is twenty, Thomas. So you tell me—what would threescore come to?"

Thomas made a face. Arithmetic caused him considerable pain.

"It seems to me," Grandfather said, "that a boy who has a mort of baseball statistics in his head should be able to cope with simple multiplication."

"It isn't the same. Stats are fun, Grandfather. Multiplication is arithmetic."

Grandfather, wagging his head, replied that no doubt he thought he was making sense.

After a minute's concentration, Thomas shouted, "Sixty!"

"And plus ten would make it—?"

"Seventy miles!"

"Right again. At this rate, you'll soon be ready for integral calculus."

"Gosh, I hope not. Is it seventy miles to Tampa?"

"No. I just thought of the poem when you asked how far we have to go."

"Well, it's a good poem, all right. So—how many miles to Tampa?"

"Twoscore and six."

Wrinkling his nose, Thomas worked it out. "Forty-six, right?"

"Right again."

"What does that mean—can they get there by candlelight yes and back again?"

"Figure it out."

Thomas frowned. "Well, probably can they get wherever it is and back before dark, huh?"

"Of course. Perhaps when that poem was written, there were only candles to use when night came on."

"Who wrote it?"

"I don't know."

This was something his grandfather almost never said, and Thomas was impressed.

"Grandfather?"

"Yes, Thomas?"

"Why do you suppose they wanted to get there and back again in such a hurry?"

"Delivering a message, maybe?"

"Could be. Or meeting somebody and bringing them back. Like us, going to Tampa, to meet Aunt Linzy at the train."

"Could be," said Grandfather, sounding sort

of glum. "Is this where we go right?"

As they scarcely ever drove far from home, Thomas looked about alertly, taking in the sights. The Tamiami Trail, Route 41, took them through small towns, past stretches of sparsely treed land, sometimes a field with cattle or horses standing about. On both sides were fruit and vegetable stands; antique shops; flea markets; U-Store U-Lock bins; used-car lots; yards full of pink plastic flamingos, iron deer, flocks of plaster ducks; monument makers displaying stone angels and granite gave slabs; lots of bars; long stretches of sheds where Ruskin tomatoes were packed for shipping; road stops where you could eat what Grandfather called grease-fried food, only they never stopped for it; different kinds of churches; phosphate mines with mountains of slag piled behind them—so ugly that Grandfather turned his head away as they passed; plenty of schools and trailer parks and condominium complexes and just plain houses.

It seemed to Thomas very crowded and busy

and interesting, and he was enjoying the ride, but Grandfather kept muttering about the traffic. Of course, it was awfully hot, so maybe by the time the trip was over he wouldn't be liking it much himself.

"You always say it's no use complaining about what you can't do anything about, Grandfather."

"You're asking me to be consistent. That's unreasonable."

"You don't like to drive, do you?"

"I do not."

Thomas, who could hardly wait to be old enough to get his license, said, "I suppose that's why we just about never go anywhere?"

"You suppose right. Why? Is there someplace you wish to go?"

Thomas shook his head. "Not really. Not yet, anyway. Pittsburgh, someday. When we have enough money."

On and on. Past Piney Point and Sun City and Ruskin and Apollo Beach. Past East Tampa.

"Now we're getting somewhere!" said

Thomas, just as Grandfather brought the pickup to a stop.

A few hundred feet ahead, a freight train moved slowly along the railroad tracks. There was a long line of cars and trucks in front of them, in the lane beside them, and—Thomas twisted around to look—stretching out behind them. Some still had their motors idling, trying to keep their air-conditioners going and making, Grandfather said, the atmosphere morbid. The pickup didn't have air-conditioning, so he turned the engine off. Hundreds of radios blared, but their own hadn't worked for years, so he and Grandfather didn't add to the noise.

From vehicles up and down the lines, drivers and passengers were getting out to stand in the moist, roasting heat and talk, and scowl, and even make fists in the direction of the train that dragged heavily past, seeming to have no end, certainly not hurried by raised fists.

"Oh, boy," Thomas said. "A lot of the people look awfully mad."

Grandfather shrugged. He was more patient

about standing still than going ahead. "Nothing to do but wait for the caboose to arrive. Does seem to be taking a deal of time to delight us with its appearance." He took his big handkerchief out and wiped his face and neck.

Thomas, sweating, sticking to the worn leather seat, said, "I'm thirsty."

"So'm I."

"It's *hot*, Grandfather."

"Certainly is."

"It's like being stuck in the middle of a hot wet *sponge!*"

"Well put."

That took care of that.

Thomas scrunched down, leaning his head back. That way he could see the sky, where clouds were piled up for miles, one behind the other, white as chalk or cotton, and not blurred together but separate and sharp in their outlines. Cloud cities in the sky, Grandfather sometimes called them, and, other times, the mountain ranges of heaven. He said that the summer skies of Florida reminded him of

48

African skies. Wide open from horizon to horizon.

Long ago, when he was a young man, before he was married to Grandmother, Grandfather had gone to Africa, to Nigeria, to Benin, the town his ancestors had been taken from centuries before, to be made slaves in the American southland. From listening to stories about it, Thomas almost felt he'd been in that wide-skied African land himself. That he could walk through those houses—open to the air, with porches all around and no screens at the windows but mosquito netting surrounding the beds. Thomas thought it would be fun to sleep surrounded by mosquito netting. Large brown and blue geckos climbed the walls and ceilings of those rooms in Benin, as lizards made free of their own rooms at home. Nigerians collected palm wine in buckets, the way people in New England got maple syrup. They fished the Niger River, as Grandfather and Thomas fished the Gulf of Mexico.

"A wide, deep, tea-colored river," Grandfather had told him. "I can see, as if it were only yesterday, fishermen casting their nets from dugouts—"

"How could they cast nets from a *dugout?*"

"Thomas! The dugout was a canoe for thousands of years before it became a pit full of ball players."

"Oh, yeah. I forgot," Thomas had said, grinning.

Now, in the broiling truck, under a sky that reminded Grandfather of Africa, they waited for the freight train to come to an end and let them travel on to Tampa and Aunt Linzy.

On a bench in the Tampa railroad station, surrounded by suitcases and cardboard boxes, was a lady clutching a large handbag, wearing a hat and coat and a discontented expression.

"Forty years," Grandfather muttered to Thomas, "and I could pick her out of thousands."

"Why?"

"For one thing, only Linzy would have on a coat and hat in Florida on a day like this. Besides, she always looked as if she expected her purse to be snatched, and she still does."

The lady was looking all around, her eyes

passing over Grandfather and Thomas, moving on to the rest of the vast depot.

"She doesn't know you after forty years, Grandfather."

"Must be my beard. Well, let's go, Thomas. Remember, we are to be—"

"Yes, Grandfather. I remember, and I will be."

They walked up to her and Grandfather bowed slightly in a way that Thomas always found pleasing.

"Linzy," he said. "Here we are. This is Thomas."

"Joseph Weaver! Are you aware that I've been waiting nearly an hour in this terrible place?"

"Sorry. We were held up by a train. By two trains, in fact. We hadn't gone three miles after getting past the first one when we were stopped by a second. Unless it was the same train going around and around like those electric Lionel sets in department stores—"

"What are you *talking* about?"

"I'm trying to explain why we are— Well, it doesn't matter now."

"It does to me. I've been waiting nearly an—"

"But we couldn't help it, Linzy. Anyway, how could we expect your train to arrive on time?"

"It was early."

"Unheard of," said Grandfather, shaking his head. "Is all of this—that is, does all this belong to you?"

"It does. I trust I won't be putting you out?"

"Oh, no. No, no. I just wasn't sure. Didn't want to take someone else's belongings. Wanted to be sure."

"Well, now you are. I hope your car isn't too far away. I don't feel up to a long walk in this heat."

"Why don't you take off your hat and coat? Anyway, your coat?"

"Easier to wear than to carry."

"In this heat?"

"Joseph. I've got along all these years without advice from you. I scarcely need it now."

Thomas, listening to this exchange, thought

it was pretty funny. They'd picked up bickering right where they'd left off all those years ago.

"Well," Grandfather said, "I'll go get the truck and bring it around to the front. Thomas, you wait here with your aunt Linzy."

"Sure, Grandfather."

When Grandfather had gone, Thomas stood in front of his great-aunt, studying her face.

"Is there something wrong?" she asked sharply.

"No, Aunt Linzy. Your purse is safe, isn't it?"

"I should think so. I keep a firm hold on it. Why do you ask?"

"I just wouldn't want it to get snatched."

"It won't be," Aunt Linzy said in a firm tone. "What's that?" she asked. "It looks like a baseball glove."

"That's what it is."

"Why are you carrying it?"

"I always do."

"Why?"

Thomas lifted his shoulders. "I just do, is all. I like to have it with me, in case."

"Do you think that a baseball will come flying through the air in a railroad depot?"

"Grandfather says nothing is impossible."

"Well, he's wrong. Just about everything is impossible."

Thomas wrinkled his nose, scratched his elbow, looked from side to side.

"Why don't you sit here beside me?" she asked.

Moving one of the suitcases, wondering how they were going to fit them and all the boxes into their house, he sat.

"How old are you, Thomas?"

"Going on eleven."

"Do you like school?"

"Some of it. Not arithmetic."

"I've been a bookkeeper all my life. I'll tutor you."

"Thank you," Thomas said unhappily.

"What are your interests?"

It was like taking a test, except he didn't care if he passed. He said, "Baseball. Fishing. I like to read, not as much as Grandfather of course, and play checkers and cribbage and do jigsaw puzzles—"

"I myself am partial to jigsaw puzzles, provided they're difficult enough."

"That's good. We always have one—"

"I understand I am putting you out of your room."

"Well. Yes."

"I'm sorry."

"It's all right," Thomas lied, wondering how much longer Grandfather was going to be. And here he came, mopping his forehead again.

Aunt Linzy stood. "I believe that among us, we can carry it all," she informed them.

They managed. At the front of the station stood the pickup. Aunt Linzy regarded it with an open mouth.

"Joseph! I can't ride in that!"

"Uh?" A pause. "It's— You have to, Linzy. It's what we came in, and it's what we have to go back in."

"I should never have sold my car."

"You did that?" Grandfather said.

56

"I did. I assumed you would have a suitable . . . Well, nothing to do about it. Poor Thomas, you'll have to ride in back with the luggage."

"No!" Grandfather snapped. "I never let Thomas ride there. It's dangerous."

"We'll be crowded."

"Isn't that the truth."

Grandfather grunted, lifting boxes and suitcases to the rear of the truck. Thomas didn't think he sounded especially gracious or understanding.

They started off, Thomas in the middle, glove on his lap. In a few minutes they were all sticking to the seat, and in a few miles arrived at a railroad crossing just as the warning signs began to swing.

"I don't believe this," said Grandfather. "We're caught in an epidemical train conspiracy!"

"Anyhow," Thomas said, "this time we got here first. We can count how many cars." He started counting.

"One hundred and twenty-three!" he said triumphantly, forty minutes later.

As they headed south again on the Tamiami Trail, Grandfather said, "Well then, Linzy. Suppose you tell me all you've said and read and thought and worn and eaten and suffered and laughed at since last we met."

"Are you trying to be funny, Joseph?"

"Well, no. I guess I was trying to be jolly."

"Your humor hasn't altered with age."

"Nor has yours, apparently," said Grandfather.

Silence for nearly a mile. Then she said, "I remained with the department store and got to be head bookkeeper. Then they introduced computers and said I was too old to learn to keep the books on them. Ridiculous."

"Of course it's ridiculous, Linzy. They forced you out?"

"As good as. Well, I have a small pension, and my Social Security. I'm independent. But it was extremely annoying to be told that I went out with the handwritten ledger."

"You could fight that, you know. There are

anti–age-discrimination laws."

"I know. I preferred not to."

"I guess you never married, or I'd have heard."

"I fail to see why you would have heard. We've hardly kept in touch."

"No. You're right there."

The question "Why are we in touch now?" was not voiced. Another silence followed before Aunt Linzy said, "I did not marry. Not that I think it's any business of yours."

Thomas thought that it certainly was Grandfather's business, and his own, too. If she'd got married, she wouldn't be riding here in this truck with them, going to stay in their house and who knew how long for.

Except, she could've got married, and then her husband died, and then she still decided to look up Grandfather that she hadn't seen in all these years but still bickered with, and be riding here in the truck with them. . . .

"Thomas," she said, "please stop wriggling. That just makes us hotter."

Thomas opened his mouth, caught a sidewise glance from his grandfather, and kept still.

After a long while with nobody speaking, she said, "Joseph! Are we almost there?"

Grandfather gave a really hearty laugh.

"What's funny, may I ask?"

"Sure you may. I thought only children said are we there yet. It just struck me as funny."

"You haven't answered the question."

"Yes, Linzy. We are almost there."

At home, Ringo came from the garden to give them his usual greeting. "Where have you been?" he muttered and mewed. "I've been all *alone* here with this cuckoo duck!"

Only this time, Thomas thought with surprise, he appeared to address his remarks to Aunt Linzy, twining his long length around her legs. Ivan dashed at Thomas's ankles, and Thomas pushed him aside with one foot.

"Thomas!" Aunt Linzy said sharply. "How can you do such a thing!"

"What did I do?"

"You kicked that goose!"

"It isn't a goose, it's a—"

"He didn't kick it, Linzy. We have to move it out of the way when it goes for our ankles. It is an exceedingly ill-humored duck."

"The poor thing," said Aunt Linzy, bending down and holding her hand out to Ivan.

Thomas held his breath, and "Don't do that—" Grandfather snapped. "He'll take your finger off—"

Ivan put his ugly bill on Aunt Linzy's outstretched palm.

"I am very very fond of dumb creatures," she said, crooning to Ivan and stroking Ringo with her free hand.

Thomas and his grandfather exchanged dumbfounded glances.

In the house, Grandfather put the suitcases in Thomas's room and told his sister-in-law that the boxes would have to be stacked on the porch for later disposition.

"Suppose it rains?" Thomas whispered.

Grandfather shrugged. "Then we'll shove them in the middle of the living room. You have another suggestion? Please don't answer that."

In his room, Thomas found Aunt Linzy removing his things from the dresser drawers, piling them neatly on the bed. When the drawers were empty, she moved to the closet and began taking his clothes out.

"But Aunt Linzy—" he began.

"We'll have to find someplace to put all this, won't we? Perhaps in your grandfather's room?"

Thomas turned on his heel. Grandfather was sitting in his chair in the living room, staring at his hands. Thomas marched over and stood, taking deep breaths, waiting for him to look up.

"What is it?" Grandfather said at last.

"She's emptied all my stuff onto the bed! From the drawers and the closet, too. She says we have to find somewhere to put it."

"She has?" Grandfather patted Thomas's shoulder and got to his feet with a long sigh. "I guess there's room in my closet to wedge your things in."

"Grandfather?"

"Thomas?"

"She's going to stay here a long time, isn't she?"

"Looks that way."

"What are we going to do?"

"We are going to be—"

"Grandfather!" Thomas said, close to tears. "I don't *feel* gracious and understanding!"

"Make a pretense, will you? Things are difficult enough. We can't have you going to pieces. I'll help carry your clothes into my room."

They found Aunt Linzy, spectacles dangling from one hand, holding the picture of Thomas's parents close to her nose. She turned and said, "How young, how young they were. Life is so . . . life is so . . ." She blinked, put the picture down, and said, "You'll take your books, too, won't you, Thomas? I'll be needing the shelves, when all my things are unpacked."

Thomas compressed his lips, so words couldn't get out.

At six o'clock, Grandfather began preparations for dinner, taking from the icebox six small fillets of trout that he had earlier dipped in milk and seasoned cornmeal. Now he was melting a mixture of oil and margarine in a skillet as Thomas set the table. For three people. As if for Donny or Mr. McCallam on a visit, he told himself. But it wasn't the same. No way. This extra place was not for somebody invited for dinner. It was for Aunt Linzy, who'd invited herself, for forever maybe—

"There," she said, coming in with Ringo at her heels. "I've done what I can for now, until we get my boxes unpacked. We can get to that tomorrow. Joseph—we don't have air-conditioning here, do we?"

Thomas saw Grandfather's jaw tighten. He said, "No. *We* do not. We have ceiling fans and ocean breezes."

"There's not a sign of a breeze."

"From yon twelve-winded sky, no breath touches this shore. Just now. Even air-conditioning gets out of whack sometimes."

"Fancy talk, just like the old days. Well, well. What can't be cured must be endured. That's what I always say. What are you doing there?"

"Getting dinner."

Aunt Linzy moved over to the stove. "Oh, dear. This won't do, Joseph."

"What won't—"

"I'm afraid that I eat neither fish nor flesh nor fowl."

Grandfather closed his eyes.

"Actually," she went on, "I find it distasteful even to watch people eating the flesh of—"

"Linzy!" Grandfather bellowed.

"Well, my goodness. You don't have to yell at me."

"I'm sorry." Clearing his throat, Grandfather continued in an irritably patient tone. "I have always respected—even admired—the attitude of vegetarians, Linzy. But Thomas and I are not of that persuasion. If—since—we are to be together for—for a while—you will have to accept that. We eat fish. We eat fowl. If you prefer, you could have your meals separate from us."

"That would be inconvenient. I suppose I can accommodate. The dear knows I frequently have to, the way so many people insist on—"

"What I can do," Grandfather interrupted, "is prepare a vegetable stir-fry for you. Would that do?"

"Very nicely."

"We already have salad ingredients, but not enough. Thomas, take the basket and go get a selection of—"

Aunt Linzy looked out the kitchen window. "I see you still garden, Joseph. That's good."

"Thomas!" Grandfather said sharply. "Did you hear me? I asked you to—"

"I'll go myself," said Aunt Linzy, removing a basket that hung on a hook by the door. "I know better what I want. For instance, radishes repeat on me. I cannot eat radishes. Or cucumbers. Cucumbers give me gas."

"We don't have any—" Grandfather was saying as she went out the door. "Who puts radishes or cucumbers in a stir-fry?" he muttered. "Sorry I snapped at you, Thomas."

"It's okay, Grandfather."

He couldn't see that anything was okay, but

he couldn't, either, see what to do about everything that was so far from being okay.

"You and I, Thomas, are going to have to be very patient. Not just with Linzy. With each other. This is a—an abrasive situation."

"What's abrasive?"

"In this case, it translates as unspeakable. So let's not speak of it."

After dinner, Aunt Linzy said she was utterly exhausted. "That wretchedly uncomfortable drive, after the long train ride. I think I'll go to bed."

"So are we," said Grandfather. "Exhausted."

"And no wonder. Probably we should all retire, so as to have tomorrow for seeing to my things."

To this neither Thomas nor Grandfather replied.

In bed—so to speak—on the couch, Thomas waited for Ringo to come and nestle beside him, as he did when Mr. McCallam was visiting, but time passed with no sign of his cat. Thomas pulled the pillow over his head and a few tears rolled down his face.

Next morning, Aunt Linzy came into the kitchen smiling. "I slept like a baby. In spite of this awful heat, and your ceiling fans are of little help, Joseph. They just move the hot air in a circle. Nevertheless—like a *baby*. I wouldn't have believed it possible. Of course, I was desperately tired, which probably accounts for it. Thomas! Your cat is delightful! He spent the entire night at the foot of my bed. I am flattered!"

Grandfather, with a quick glance at Thomas, said, "It's the room he's used to, of course."

Thomas, with an ache in his throat, turned away. "I'm going over to Donny's."

"You haven't had breakfast—"

"I don't want any. I'll—I'll be back—sometime."

A week later, Thomas and Donny were eating cones in a yogurt shop.

"It's not going so good, huh?" said Donny.

Thomas shrugged.

"Did you get all her boxes unpacked?"

"Some of them. Grandfather told her we'd have to put the rest in a storage place. There isn't enough *room* for it all."

"Did Grandfather get a cot for you in his room, like he said?"

"Yes."

"Don't you want to talk?"

"Yes."

"So?"

Thomas burst out, "She's cleaning the whole place. I mean, the cards and checkers and dominoes and we had a Scrabble game halfway done and she just swept all the tiles into the bag, and *everything's* in drawers now, she says we can get them out when we play but isn't it tidier to tidy them away when we aren't. And Grandfather caught her just in time before she cleared all our shells and bottle glass and even the fossil into a box. . . ."

A day or two after her arrival, Grandfather and Thomas had come in from a morning on the beach to find Aunt Linzy sitting near the bookshelves with one of her boxes on the floor beside her. She was wrapping in tissue paper, then putting in the box, all their shells, bottle glass, beachstone figures, the smaller pieces of sculpture. She was clearing from their shelves years and years of treasures.

"Linzy!" Grandfather shouted. "What the deuce are you doing?"

"As you see, Joseph. I am carefully packing your collection of—" She picked up the fossil. "Goodness, I remember this. You've had it for ages, haven't you. I think I remember Marta showing it to—"

"Why are you packing our things?"

"For safekeeping, of course. And to make room."

"They've been safe enough where they are all these years. I do not think they'll be safer in a— Room for what?"

"There is, Joseph, the matter of *my* possessions. I've only been able to empty this one box, and there are all the others on the porch. I don't think I'll be able to get much more in my room—"

Thomas swallowed hard to keep himself

from saying, "*Whose* room?" He didn't dare look at Grandfather.

"So? What happened?" Donny asked.

"Grandfather made her—I mean, asked her—to put our stuff back, and they had a—a talk—about her boxes on the porch. She got a lot of the stuff out, and the rest we've put in a U-Store U-Lock over on Cortez. She says she's going to buy another dresser to put in my room. Except she calls it her room. She says she's going to tutor me in arithmetic, when school starts. So she's going to be here then. When it starts. I think she'll still be here when I get to high school. I think she's moved *in*. Period."

"Gee. It sounds—" Donny finished his cone, wiped his mouth, and asked gently, like a doctor touching a sore spot, "What about Ringo—I mean, is he—"

"She's taken him over, too. Her room, her cat. It'll be her house, probably, pretty soon."

"Oh, that's not so, Thomas. I mean, Ringo. He's *always* been your cat."

71

"Not anymore. Grandfather says I must make allowances for feline vagaries."

"What're they?"

"Dumb stupid ideas."

"Really?"

"No, not really."

"Grandfather knows lots of fancy words."

"He reads lots of books. You know what else he says? He says I should be *glad* that Ringo has made another friend. That's supposed to make me feel better. If you ask *me*," Thomas continued bitterly, "he's a traitor. That's what he is."

"Grandfather?"

"Don't be dumb. Ringo. He's turned against me."

"Gosh, Thomas—that's awful. How are you going to stand it, having her there, I mean—living with you?"

Thomas lifted his shoulders. "She's gotta live somewhere, I suppose."

"You know something?"

"Probably not."

"That's what you said about Ivan one time. You said he's gotta live somewhere."

"So—they both gotta, and we're stuck with them. And that fool Ivan is as bad as Ringo. Follows her around like she was the rainbow the pot of gold is at the end of."

"Funny."

"What's *funny*?"

"How animals like her. Maybe it makes up to her for you and Grandfather not liking her."

"What's that supposed to mean?"

"I don't know," Donny said in confusion. "I guess it doesn't mean anything."

"Nothing means anything. Let's get our bikes and go for a long ride."

"Okay."

"GOODNESS," SAID AUNT LINZY, coming into the living room on an afternoon in late August. "Is that game still going on?" Grandfather held up a shushing hand. The score was tied in the bottom of the tenth, game at Wrigley Field, Cubs batter up, count no balls, two strikes, a man on first with two out. . . .

"Well, really! I was only going to say—"

Andre Dawson, with a line single to left, drove in the winning run and Grandfather turned the radio off.

"If their pitching doesn't fall apart," he said, "Chicago might actually win the division. Who'd have thought it, in spring training?"

"In spring training," Thomas said glumly, "I

was *sure* the Pirates would."

Aunt Linzy said brightly, "I looked in the paper this morning, to see the boxing scores—"

"Box scores," Grandfather muttered.

"Oh really, Joseph. I am trying to take an interest."

"It is not necessary, Linzy. Really. Thomas and I understand that baseball isn't your sport."

Jigsaw puzzles, thought Thomas. That's her sport. She finished puzzles he and Grandfather had started, without asking if they minded. Thomas minded. By herself, she did the three hard ones a lot faster than he and Grandfather, together, could do the kind that had scenery.

"I believe," she was saying, "that family members should have interests in common. That's why I'm trying to understand the fascination of baseball even if it seems to me shocking that men get such ridiculous salaries for playing what is a—"

"Child's game. Yes, Linzy. That's been said many times. But believe me, we don't in the *least* wish to impose our pastimes on you."

We don't, Thomas thought, want to share baseball with you. Or fishing—which anyway Aunt Linzy wouldn't dream of sharing. Or our house. Or Ringo.

Ringo came in from the kitchen, briefly brushed along Thomas's leg, sprang to Aunt Linzy's lap. For Thomas, after all these weeks it still felt like a punch in the heart when Ringo, his own cat that had been his from a kitten he'd rescued from the rain, showed that he preferred somebody else. Ringo didn't absolutely ignore him, but if Aunt Linzy was in the room, to her he went. Every time.

"According to the boxing—I mean, *box* scores—your team, the Philadelphia Pirates, is sixteen games out of first place."

"Pittsburgh."

"What?"

"Pittsburgh Pirates."

"Of course. I mix them up."

Grandfather muttered, close to Thomas's ear, "She only does it to annoy, because she knows it teases."

76

Thomas was sure of that. Aunt Linzy was a lot of things, only dumb wasn't one of them. She knew baseball terms by now, but mixed them up on purpose. To show she was too good for it? To make him and Grandfather look silly, being crazy about a kid's game? Who knew why she did it, or why she did any of the other things that she'd been doing since she got here.

Like ironing sheets and underwear.

One day, shortly after she'd moved in, Aunt Linzy said, "I can't find your ironing board, Joseph."

"We don't have one."

"How do you iron things?"

"When we do—which is practically never—we put a blanket and a sheet on the kitchen table. Works fine."

"For my part, I think beautifully pressed clothes and bed linen are very important."

"I see. All right, I'll get an ironing board."

"Good. From now on, you can leave the laundering to me. It's the least I can do."

"That is not necess—"

"Nonsense. It will be my pleasure."

Thomas and Grandfather found their shirts, trousers, underwear, and sheets pressed and neatly stacked on their beds each week.

"Do you suppose she'd iron my sneakers if I asked?" Thomas said.

"Please. Spare me." Later Grandfather said to Aunt Linzy, "The sheets are supposed to be no-iron."

"There's no such thing. You must admit that unwrinkled bed linen is much pleasanter to sleep on."

Grandfather admitted nothing of the kind, but didn't protest. Nor did he say much when Aunt Linzy, using the sewing machine she'd brought with her, made curtains, and then slipcovers to match.

"There!" she exclaimed, when the job was finished. "Doesn't that look much nicer than blank windows and that tattered old upholstery?"

"It's pretty," Grandfather said, and added, "Thank you, Linzy."

"My pleasure."

Aunt Linzy always said, "My pleasure," when she made improvements that Thomas didn't always think improved things. Like the vacuum cleaner she bought. He and Grandfather had never had one, because they had no rugs. But Aunt Linzy found ways to use it every few days. She was bothered at how sand got tracked into the house, so she put sisal mats just inside the kitchen and front doors. They already had them on the outside. She asked, once, if it wouldn't be a good idea for them to remove their shoes before coming in the house, but Grandfather said they weren't living in Japan, and that was that.

Aunt Linzy was a good cook, and made dinner two or three times a week, using lots of vegetables and pasta. She made soup with things from the stir-fry garden, or even fruit, that Grandfather said was as good as any he made with soup bones.

She had made, in the time she'd been with them, lots of changes in their house, in their lives. Grandfather, trying to look on the sunny side, said it wasn't all bad, now was it, Thomas?

They were sitting on the front-porch swing, Ringo on his railing perch, listening to the evening choir of birds. Aunt Linzy had gone to visit Mrs. Price. They'd become vegetarian friends and exchanged recipes about how to make turnips exciting and amaze people with tofu. Or make soup from plums.

"Plum soup," Thomas said irritably. "That's crazy."

"Tasted pretty good, didn't it?"

Thomas wriggled. "I suppose."

"Do you want to talk about it, Thomas?"

"About what?"

"Now, now. You know about what."

"What's to say?"

"I know how difficult this is being for you. But don't you think it *could* be worse?"

"How?"

"Well—Ivan doesn't bite us anymore. There's that."

"Hah-hah."

After a short silence, Grandfather said,

"Your aunt Linzy has a good disposition, which is nothing to hah-hah about. Too many people are constantly whining and complaining about their lot in life. You must admit your aunt is usually pretty cheerful."

"And I think it's funny."

"What do you mean?"

"Grandfather. If you lived someplace where people were wondering how much longer you were going to stay, would you be cheerful? I wouldn't be. I'd be—" He hesitated.

"What would you be?"

Grumpy, Thomas started to say, but changed his mind. "Sad, I guess."

"Thomas, tell me. Have you once tried to look at this situation from your aunt's point of view instead of your own?"

"No. Have you?"

"Yes. Could you try?"

"No."

Grandfather continued to have the waiting look he got when he expected something more from Thomas.

"She took my room away from me."

"We're making out all right in mine, aren't we?"

"It isn't that, Grandfather—"

"I know." He held up one hand. "You needn't say what you're thinking. But *I* am thinking of what people all over the world have to endure that you and I do not. Millions of human beings hungry, hopeless, frightened. *Homeless*, Thomas. Nowhere to *live*. You and I just have to put up for a while with one lonely old lady."

"What does 'for a while' mean? I don't think it's for a while. I think she's *living* with us."

"Thomas, Thomas. You don't often disappoint me. But sometimes you do, really you do. If that should be the case—what do you suggest? Tell her to pack up and get out?"

"She stole my cat."

Thomas looked at Ringo, beautiful and composed on the railing. It made his throat, and his heart, really ache—the way Ringo had left him for Aunt Linzy.

Grandfather put an arm over Thomas's shoulders and pulled him close.

"Things never can remain the same,

Thomas. It's the way life is. . . . Everything changes, and we can't stop that."

Thomas sighed. Grandfather always knew what he was thinking. "You don't bicker with her anymore, do you?"

"No. It would make things worse."

"I'm not being a good sport, am I?"

"Not especially."

"I don't want to disappoint you, Grandfather."

"I know that."

"I'll try to be better."

"Good. How about a game of Scrabble before we go to bed?"

"Okay. I mean, I'd like that."

They went into the living room, to the games table, got the Scrabble set from the drawer where Aunt Linzy had stored it, and set up.

Ringo followed, leaping to Thomas's lap. He settled down and began to run his motor. Thomas, one hand on the large silky head, thought how impossible it was to hold a grudge against a cat. The same as they didn't hold grudges against people.

"A solid and sagacious cat," said Grandfather.

"I know," Thomas said. "What's sagacious?"

"Wise."

"Why don't you just say 'wise'?"

"Oh—I like to let the odd word in now and then. Makes conversation more interesting."

"Is Ringo sagacious to leave me for somebody else, after all I've done for him?"

Grandfather laughed. "It has nothing to do with sagacity or with what you've done for him. He's having a flirtation. Believe me, wisdom goes out the window when flirtation comes in the door. It won't last forever. Ringo knows you're his best friend."

"I guess," said Thomas, wondering if he believed it or just wanted to. Either way, he loved Ringo. He supposed that was what counted.

Reaching in the bag, he pulled out a "Z" and stared in astonishment. "That has *never* happened to me before! I never got a 'Z' first crack out of the bag in my whole entire life before!"

"In your whole entire life, Thomas. Think of

it!" Grandfather picked an "E" and pretended to scowl.

When Aunt Linzy came in, Thomas looked up and smiled at her. It made his mouth feel stiff, but she seemed pleased.

"Well, there you are!" she said. "And my pussycat, too, sitting on Thomas's lap. I'm jealous!"

Grandfather got to his feet, yawning. "We'll finish this tomorrow, eh? And Linzy—*don't* put our game away, hear?"

Thomas, following Grandfather to their shared room, said, "You broke up the game so Ringo wouldn't leave me and go to her, didn't you?"

"Nonsense. I'm just tired."

In bed, hands beneath his head, Thomas thought that probably nobody else in the world had someone to live with as wonderful—and as sagacious—as his grandfather. It made up for also having Aunt Linzy to live with. And put up with.

"Good night, Grandfather," he said in the dark.

"Pleasant dreams, Thomas."

"See you in the morning."

Presently Grandfather's gentle snore began, and from the reaches of the night came the call of a hunting owl. Thomas loved to hear owls, though he was sorry for small creatures, crouching frozen with fear at sounds he thought beautiful. Sometimes you heard a rabbit scream as it was carried away through the dark, and that was bad. Sad. Just the same— owls were mysterious marvelous birds, and they had to eat too, and feed their babies.

Thomas knew the different species by their calls. The flutey flutter of a screech owl, the bark of the barred owl, the sort of hiss that the barn owl gave, and the long, lonely *hoo, hoo-hoo-hoo, hoo-oo* of the great horned owl, the one that was out there now, cruising the night.

Suddenly, to Thomas's joy, Ringo came into the room and leaped up to settle purring in the crook of his knees, as if he had never left this bed for another.

By THE SECOND WEEK IN September the Cubs
were five games up in the eastern division.
Thomas and Grandfather had put Pittsburgh
on hold to get behind Chicago for the pennant
race, and were listening to a night game at
Wrigley Field. Joe Girardi, the Cubs' catcher,
had got an infield single off Kevin Gross, scoring Vance Law from third, to take the game
from Montreal.

"A sweep!" said Grandfather, reaching to
turn off the radio. "A fine and final sweep!"

"Final?" Aunt Linzy looked up with a trace of
hope.

"I meant, Linzy, that it's the last time we face the Expos, and we swept them."

"Oh. Who's we?"

"The Chicago Cubs."

"You change hats pretty often, don't you? I thought it was all Pittsburgh for you two."

"We'll go back to the Pirates next year, but we have to be realistic, and right now the Cubs are leading the National League, and that's what matters."

Aunt Linzy was looking very hot and tired. Her hair straggled in damp wisps. She dabbed at her face and neck with a man's handkerchief. She'd even pushed Ringo from her lap, telling him it was too hot.

"Wouldn't you think in September it would begin to cool off a trifle? In Chicago, by this time of year the air is lovely and crisp—"

"I know," Grandfather said. "The ivy's getting brown on the outfield wall."

"What *are* you talking about?"

"Wrigley Field, Linzy. At the start of the season, the ivy looks lifeless on the outfield wall, but—*'lo! and be whole'*—as April passes, you see a green leaf here and there, and then more and more, and finally the entire wall is beautifully green and ivied. Of course, it begins to shrivel again as the season winds down—"

"Winds down? Does the season ever do that?"

"Poor Linzy," Grandfather said. "I know this is being hard on—"

"How long does it *take*, the whole business?"

"Well. There's spring training. There are one hundred and sixty-two games in the regular season, not counting the All-Star break, which I'd be willing to eliminate. Then the play-offs. Then the World Series."

"But that's practically the entire year!"

Grandfather stroked his beard. "You could look at it that way."

"What possible other way—"

"It'll be over soon, I promise. By the middle of October, for sure."

"And this is only the middle of September." She ran her tongue over her lips. "I think I'll make some lemonade."

"That would be very nice."

When she'd gone to the kitchen, Grandfather and Thomas looked at each other.

"Gosh," said Thomas, wrinkling his nose.

"Yes."

"But—what can we do?"

"Nothing. I do feel sorry for her."

After a moment, Thomas said, "I do, too. But it kind of—not really, but sort of—takes some of the fun out, doesn't it?"

"The way of the world, Thomas. The way of the world."

"You always say that."

"And always mean what I say."

After a moment, Thomas said, "Do you think we'll ever get the television fixed? So we can maybe see Bobby Bonilla, or the ivy on the outfield wall? So we can look at some games again?"

"Oh, I expect so. Someday."

"I see." Someday didn't mean tomorrow. "By the World Series?"

"Maybe. Not saying for sure which year."

"I see."

Aunt Linzy came in with a frosty pitcher and

three glasses that she'd put in the freezer to coat with an icy mist. "Here we are!" she said brightly. "I tell you what, boys. I've decided that since I can't lick you, I must join you. Next year I shall root right beside you for the—well, I'll be for whatever team you're for. You do seem to keep changing your minds. I shall read up on the game during the winter, so as to be prepared! What do you say to that!"

Thomas's heart dropped to his feet like a botched bunt, and Grandfather took a deep breath before he smiled and said, "That's sporting of you, Linzy."

In silence they swallowed the cold drink that was sweet and tart and had little chips of ice in it to brush the lips.

"Delicious," said Grandfather, putting his glass down.

"Yeah," said Thomas. "It's great, Aunt Linzy."

"My pleasure," she said. "Now, tell me, so we can start my lessons right away—does the person who is at the—the mound it's called?—yes, of course, the mound . . . does that person throw the ball or is he the one trying to hit it?"

Grandfather grabbed the end of his nose. Thomas put his head on his knees.

"If you aren't going to help," she said, looking from one to the other, "I don't see how I can learn."

"Reading's a good idea, Linzy. I'll lend you some of my books. You can learn a lot that way."

"Well, I really would've thought—" A pause, and then, "All right. If that's the way you're going to be, I'll read about it." She emptied her glass, made a move to rise, sank back. "You two don't seem interested in your other so-called sport lately."

"What so-called sport is that?" Grandfather inquired.

"Fishing of course. You've almost stopped fishing. Why is that?"

"Too hot," said Grandfather.

"I thought you didn't mind hot weather."

"We don't. The fish do."

"Are you saying that fish feel the heat?"

"I am."

"For the dear's sake, what can they do about it?"

"Move out to deeper water. That's why we can't fish. There's nothing to catch except minnows, fry, that sort of thing. Nothing to eat. They'll be back with cooler weather."

"Then you can go after them again."

"Yes, Linzy. However much you disapprove, we'll be fishing again, come cool weather."

"Cool weather," she said, patting her cheeks, her brow, the back of her neck with the handkerchief. "There is such a thing in Florida?"

"Sometimes," said Thomas, "it's *cold*. We have to have a fire in the stove."

"When can I look for that happy circumstance?"

"Not till after Christmas," he said grumpily. No way around it. Aunt Linzy was with them for good.

Now she rose, took the tray to the kitchen, and went out the back door.

"Going to give Ivan a treat, I guess," said Grandfather.

"I guess. Grandfather?"

"Yes, Thomas?"

Thomas sighed. "Nothing."

The next day, when Thomas and Grandfather came home from marketing, their arms loaded with groceries, Ringo followed them up the porch steps to the kitchen door, where he dithered on the sill.

"What shall I do, what *shall* I do?" he asked, twining between Grandfather's legs. "Go in? Stay out?" He could not make up his mind. "Oh, help, *me-wow!* I can't decide!" he cried.

Grandfather put his bags on the counter, held the door patiently. "There are few things in life," he said to Thomas, "that can be absolutely relied upon, but one is that no cat will cross the doorsill without weighing the pros and cons. At length. Ringo! Make up your mind! Thomas, the phone's ringing."

Picking up the telephone, Thomas heard a familiar and welcome voice. "Oh, hi, Mr. McCallam." He held the receiver out. "It's Mr. McCallam, Grandfather."

Summertimes, communication between Grandfather and his friend almost stopped. Partly because the tourist season was as busy then as in winter. Mr. McCallam's motel was always full, and Chet was away in Glacier Park. Mr. McCallam hadn't found anyone else he wanted to leave the motel in the charge of.

"However," he'd said once, "that just might be arranged, and is not the real reason I avoid your place from the All-Star break until the middle of October."

Grandfather had declined to ask the real reason, but Mr. McCallam told anyway. "I'm terrified of going into extra innings and never getting out."

"Theoretically, Milo, that's possible. As the game can't end in a tie, it *could* go on forever."

"Well, Thomas," Mr. McCallam said now, "I thought I'd drive over the last weekend in October, when I presume we'll have put baseball in mothballs for a few months. I shall arrive ready to try our luck from the boat, from the pier, from the shore. I shall also expect an assortment of broiled fish, gumbos, creoles, and some rousing games of three-handed cribbage come evening. I plan to skunk the two of you. Thought I'd give you ample warning," he said confidently.

"Just a sec, Mr. McCallam." Thomas looked across the room. Ringo had apparently decided not to come in and the door was closed. "You better talk, Grandfather."

Grandfather took the phone, listened a moment, said, "Be looking forward to it, Milo." He hung up.

"You didn't sound awfully welcoming," Thomas complained.

"He took me off guard. I've never told him about Linzy's—about her visit."

Thomas and Grandfather had stopped asking each other whether Aunt Linzy might come to breakfast one morning and say, "Well, this has been very nice, and you mustn't think I haven't enjoyed it, but I have other things to do, so if you'll get the train schedule out, Joseph . . . "

It's almost, Thomas thought, as if this is the

way it's always been. As if he and Grandfather and Ringo had never had a life together, just the three of them. . . .

"You didn't tell him about Aunt Linzy at all?" he asked.

"I may have mentioned it ages ago, when she first wrote about coming. Maybe not. I can't remember."

"But what about Mr. McCallam? I mean, are we going to tell him he can't come, all on account of—"

"Of course not."

"He says he wants to play rousing games of three-handed cribbage. He says he's going to skunk us. I mean, Grandfather—how can we play three-handed cribbage with Aunt Linzy right there in the room—"

"We'll play teams. You and me against them. We'll double-skunk them, right?"

Thomas lifted his shoulders. "Where's he going to sleep?"

"Thomas, please go and find something to do. Somewhere else."

"Yes, but—"

"I have to think, don't I?"

"Yes, but what are we going to—"

"Thomas! Go to Donny's. Go to your room and read. Go out and tell Ivan what we think of him, and remember to put feeling in it."

"I don't have a room to go to, and Ivan sure knows what we think of him. How about I sleep on the sofa and Mr. McCallam uses my cot?"

Grandfather clutched his beard. "I really don't fancy bunking in with Milo, and I don't think he'd— What a darn *nuisance* everything is."

"The way of the world, Grandfather. The way of the world."

"Isn't your aunt Linzy helping Mrs. Price make mango chutney?"

"Yeah."

"Why don't you go over there and offer to help."

"How?"

"Thomas! Peel mangos, chop nuts, turn cartwheels—"

"Okay, Grandfather."

———

"So, what'll happen, do you suppose?" Donny asked.

They were sitting on his porch steps, eating cookies, their offer of help with the chutney having been declined.

"Grandfather says he's thinking. But what'll happen is I go back on the sofa and Grandfather and Mr. McCallam bunk in together and hate it. It'll maybe spoil the weekend. Ah gee, Donny—I get so *mad*."

"Yeah."

They kicked their heels in silence for a while, and then Thomas said, "You know what Aunt Linzy's gonna do, during the play-offs and the Series?"

"What?"

"Paint the house."

Donny gaped. "No kidding?"

"No kidding."

Aunt Linzy had said at dinner a few nights before that if it was all right with the two of them, she planned to occupy herself usefully while the end of the baseball season took place.

"Funny way to put it," Grandfather said. "And you always occupy yourself usefully, so far as I can see. What do you have in mind this time?"

"I shall paint the house."

Grandfather looked around the room. "You think it needs it?" he asked. "I mean, Linzy—we'll be listening to the games, and if you're trying to paint all around us, it'd be sort of diffi—"

"Not the inside. Though it does, of course, need it. No, I propose to paint the outside."

Grandfather blew out a long breath. "Whew! My goodness. Are you up to that? That's a—" Thomas was pretty sure he'd started to say "a man's job," but he changed it to "an awfully big job."

"Joseph, this place isn't much larger than a toolshed." She waved a hand. "I've painted larger structures than this."

"You are full of surprises, Linzy. You surely are."

―――――――

"She's full of surprises," Thomas said now to Donny.

"Boy, is she. She's going to paint the whole entire outside of the house?"

"She says it's hardly bigger than a toolshed," Thomas grumbled. "I didn't know she'd noticed."

"So she'll do the job all by herself?" Donny persisted.

"I guess we'll help, when we can. When there isn't a game on."

"Yeah, I know," said Donny, who liked baseball but not as much as track meets and basketball. "Pirates are hot lately," he said, to show solidarity.

"Lately is right. Too late."

"Time to go, Thomas," said Aunt Linzy, coming out on the porch.

Thomas got to his feet. "Okay, Aunt Linzy. See you, Donny."

"See you."

As they walked home, Aunt Linzy said, "You have a very good friend in Donny, don't you."

"Sure do."

"You're in the same grade?"

"Yup."

"You haven't mentioned school once since it started."

"What's to mention?"

"Do you like it?"

Thomas shrugged.

"Tell me, Thomas, because I do want to know. How do you get along there?"

"Okay. Well, arithmetic's a pain."

"I've offered to help you with that, haven't I?"

"Yes." After a second he added, "I'm going to try to catch on by myself for a little bit yet. I think I'm getting a toehold. But thanks."

"I wasn't asking for thanks. And I wasn't asking about arithmetic."

"Oh?" He'd figured that.

"That's all you have to tell me?"

Thomas scuffed his shoes, lifted his shoulders. "Everything's okay, Aunt Linzy. Really."

"I suppose I shouldn't expect an answer. I guess you think I'm snoopy."

"Oh, no, Aunt Linzy. It's nice of you to care."

"What does that mean?" she burst out. "How could I not care?"

"No, no. . . . What I meant— It's nice of you to ask. Only you don't have to worry, honest."

"That's what you think," she said sharply.

Thomas didn't ask what she meant, and was glad when they got home and could separate until suppertime.

GRANDFATHER HAD A FRIEND, Cal Grissom, who owned a twenty-foot fishing boat that could go miles out on the Gulf of Mexico, which their own small boat, of course, could not. Grandfather said he could feel her gulping before she'd gone a mile, and bailing was part of life aboard her.

Three or four times a year Mr. Grissom phoned to ask if Grandfather wanted to go with him after fish that you couldn't catch in the bay . . . Spanish mackerel, amberjack, shark, bonito, grouper, kingfish . . .

With a good day's catch, Grandfather could fill their freezer with food for weeks.

On Friday the weather continued unseasonably (Aunt Linzy said "unreasonably," but Grandfather said you couldn't ask reason of Nature) hot. When Mr. Grissom called, he said that he and a couple of other fellows were going out early the next morning, and did Grandfather want to come along.

"Sure thing, Cal. Milo? He's not here, says he's afraid of going into extra innings. I know, I know—that's what he always says. See you at the dock? Five o'clock? Good."

Hanging up, Grandfather turned and said, "That was Cal Grissom, Thomas. He's says they're going out to deep waters where the fish are. He says there's a mackerel bonanza out on the reefs—"

"Super!"

"You realize, Thomas, that children aren't invited, or you would certainly— That is, I wouldn't want you to think I'd desert you."

"Grandfather. You always say that. I think it's good for you to have a day out there with the grown-ups."

"Why do you give me the feeling, sometimes, that we've reversed ages?"

"Search me," said Thomas.

"You say you're going where the fish are?" Aunt Linzy asked. "You mean, chase them down?"

"Well, Linzy—"

"They manage to escape the heat, and escape people like you for a little while—so you take a boat and go after them?"

"Well, Linzy—"

"That's what you do, isn't it?"

"We can't fish where there are no fish. And there are some Thomas and I can't ever catch. Grouper, bonito, blackfin, Spanish mackerel . . . the sort of fish that doesn't come so close inshore. So yes. We go out after them."

"Have you ever thought what it would be like to suffocate, Joseph? Do you understand that when you catch a fish, it drowns in air, as you would dro—"

"Listen, Linzy—"

"When you and your fellow—*sportsmen*—pull a fish out of water and leave it strangling in air, you are letting it suffocate. A most unpleasant way to go, wouldn't you say, Joseph?"

"What I say is this. Men—and women—have been fishing since the world began. And I say that there aren't many pleasant deaths, and small fish getting eaten by larger fish probably don't reflect as they slide down the shark's throat, 'Well, hey now, ain't *this* the catfish's whiskers—' "

"You're deliberately avoiding my point—"

"I am not. I am answering it. I am sorry for every creature that some other creature kills or eats, but all us creatures have to eat, and fishing, for Thomas and me, is one way of getting food, getting it fresh and cheap. Furthermore, we do not let them suffocate—we keep the catch on stringers in the water until I'm ready to fillet—"

"You *enjoy* fishing!"

Thomas, his mouth open, looking from one to the other, saw that his grandfather was getting angry.

"Linzy, let me tell you something. You are not going to ruin the pleasure of fishing for

Thomas and me. Because yes, we enjoy it. And we don't have to give you explanations or apologies. I'll point out that it's not an entirely unequal contest, that fish often throw the hook—"

"Oh, I *see*. Once in a while some poor fish gets away, and that excuses you for all those that don't."

"I'm not *making* excuses—"

"I suppose you also hunt animals with a gun?"

"As it happens, no—I do not. I would never use a gun, and I despise hunting—"

"Just exactly what is the diff—"

"I don't know. I can't explain. I don't think I am obliged to explain. You take it pretty calmly when Ringo's hunting a mouse or a baby rabbit, don't you."

"That's his instinct, it's nothing he can—"

"It has been the instinct of man to fish since the dawn of creation. It was Isaak Walton's instinct, and he wrote a beautiful book about it, which maybe you ought to read. It is *my* instinct to fish, and one I've passed along to Thomas.

That's final. And I will not have you bad-mouthing it to Thomas behind my back. I will *not* have it. Is that clear?"

"Oh, yes! Yes, of course. Everything you say is *quite* clear, since you're the boss and you own this house where I'm an unwelcome intruder—"

Grandfather threw up both hands. "Time out, Linzy! Take a moment to think what you're saying. You know you're not an in-trud—"

"I know nothing of the kind." She spun on Thomas. "You tell me! Am I a welcome visitor, or are both of you just waiting for me to leave?"

"No, Aunt Linzy—"

"What do you mean, *no?* That was an either/or question. You can't answer an either/or question by saying no!"

Grandfather dropped to his chair with a groan. Thomas bit his lip and looked at the floor. Aunt Linzy ran from the room, sobbing.

Thomas walked over and stood next to his grandfather. "What do we do now?" he asked.

"Consarn it! How should I know? I'm really,

really sorry this happened. How *did* it happen?"

"You and Mr. Grissom are going where the fish are."

"Ah. Oh, yes. Should have kept my mouth shut."

"But she says that about fishing all the time."

"This time things got out of hand. Your aunt went too far, and I reacted too strongly. Thomas, let this be a lesson to you. *Think* before you speak. Always! 'A word is dead when it is said, some say. I say it just begins to live that day.' "

"Poem, huh?"

"Fine poem. Also words to live by."

"Is she going to stay in there crying all day, do you think?"

"We can't have that."

"You said she has such a good nature."

"No one can be good-natured all the time. That would be unnatural."

"I guess." After a pause, Thomas said tentatively, "There's a show at the planetarium in

Bradenton. It's about Voyager II—"

"And?" said Grandfather as their eyes met.

"Well." Thomas sniffled, rubbed his nose with the back of his hand, accepted the handkerchief that Grandfather handed him silently. "Well. I was thinking—maybe it might be interesting to go see that show."

"I should think it would be. And?"

"I was going to ask if you and I could. Before Mr. Grissom called, I was thinking of maybe asking if we could go tomorrow, since it's Oakland and Seattle playing and we wouldn't have wanted to listen to them, would we—"

"So—what are you thinking of doing instead?"

Thomas gestured with his head toward the closed bedroom door.

"Do you think if I asked, she'd take me? Her and I could do something, the two of us together."

"*She* and I, Thomas."

"If you want to go instead of I, that's okay," Thomas said, grinning.

Grandfather pulled him close in a brief hug. "In my opinion, Thomas, *you* are the catfish's whiskers!"

Very early on Saturday morning, with Aunt Linzy at the wheel, they drove Grandfather to the dock. It was dark still, though the eastern sky showed signs of a streaky dawn. *Fancy Free*, her cabin alight, rocked gently up and down on the mist-layered water. Mr. Grissom stood on deck, waving.

Grandfather got his gear from the back of the truck, turned, and said, "Now, the two of you have a fine trip through space." He looked at the sky for a moment, and said, "Should be a good day for it."

Thomas grinned. "Hey, Joe!" Cal Grissom shouted. "Come on! Let's get out there ahead of the commuters!"

"Right with you," Grandfather hollered back. He trotted down the dock, waving backward over his head.

"It was kind of you to suggest this," Aunt Linzy

said that afternoon as she and Thomas drove toward Bradenton and the planetarium.

Thomas wriggled uncomfortably. "I wanted to see the show," he muttered.

"Just the same. I appreciate being the one you want to see it with."

Thomas slapped a fist in his fielder's glove. When Aunt Linzy was this way—sort of anxious and apologetic—it bothered him more than when she was bossy, and already he was wishing their day together was over, that they'd seen the show and got home to find Grandfather in the kitchen cleaning fish.

"Where do we turn?" she asked.

"Not yet. Pretty soon. I'll tell you when."

There were other ways to get to the planetarium, but he chose to route them past McKechnie Field. There it loomed, bleachers empty against the sky, box office window boarded up, and the sign reading "Southern Home of the Pittsburgh Pirates . . . World Champions 1909, 1925, 1960, 1971, 1979" looking as if it needed a paint job.

The Pirates would be World Champions

again someday, and there'd be another year added to the sign, but just now it gave Thomas a feeling of—of loss—seeing it all so silent and deserted this way.

"That's McKechnie Field," he said, pointing.

"My goodness!" She slowed. "That's the field where you watch your team do its spring training? Not very big, is it?"

"It's cozy. I like it lots."

"Of course you do," Aunt Linzy said, picking up speed as they got past the stadium. She drove faster, and better, than Grandfather did. Both Thomas and Grandfather admitted it.

At the planetarium they sat well toward the back, although Aunt Linzy said these places were designed to let you see perfectly from anywhere in the auditorium.

The seats reclined, so that people didn't have to tip their heads back, but Aunt Linzy gave a little moan when she lay back and immediately sat up.

"Something wrong?" Thomas asked.

"Oh, dear. Thomas, I am an old lady, with an

old lady's various ills and aches and one of them is in my neck. I have arthritis in my neck. It hurts too much to lean back this way. I should have brought a pillow."

"Gee, that's a shame. You never said about your arthritis."

"What would be the point? I have it, I take pills, there's no point in talking about it. But I'm sorry, dear. I cannot lean back this way. I shall have to go outside and wait, but I don't want you to miss—"

"How about putting my glove under your neck? Would that be like a pillow, maybe?"

Aunt Linzy made a sound like a combination of laughing and crying. "Give it to me, Thomas. I'll try."

Carefully she leaned back again, the fielder's glove beneath her neck. "Perfect," she said, still with that catch in her voice. "Just perfect." For a moment she took his hand, then released it quickly. "Thank you, Thomas."

He was spared having to reply as the auditorium darkened, music began, and above them a sky brilliant with stars appeared, just like a real sky at night.

For an hour, motionless in this small room, with a man's voice for guide, they hurtled through space. A vast and looming Jupiter approached them, whirling in scarves of colored gasses, displaying its four largest moons with wonderful names that Thomas tried to memorize but immediately forgot. On toward Saturn, with its perfect rings, spinning in the dark void like a lighted top. Then Uranus appeared. Finally, at the rim of the solar system, they reached Neptune with its icy blue-and-pink moon Triton. After that, said the guiding voice, Voyager II would leave the solar system forever, steering into the reaches of interstellar space, where, failing some galactic accident, it could travel forever in a universe without end. . . .

Thomas found it all impossible to frame in his mind. Billions of years, trillions of miles. Electrical storms, bigger than three or four earths combined, that lasted for *centuries*, and had winds of over five hundred miles an hour. There was no way to get stats like that into his head. He was glad when the show ended and he and Aunt Linzy walked out of the dark reaches of space onto the sunny familiar sidewalks of Bradenton.

Grandfather was putting the last of his catch in the freezer when they got home. Aunt Linzy went to her room, saying she'd be only a moment, and Grandfather said hurriedly, "A-one trip, Thomas. The limit on mackerel and kingfish, a fourteen-pound grouper, and a string of sheepshead. We're all set for—" He broke off as Linzy came back. "Well, well, Thomas. Tell me about space travel. Did you and your aunt reach Neptune?"

"We sure did. It was great! You should see it, Grandfather. You really should. It's—awesome. Better than that, only I can't think how to say it. I kept wishing you were with us."

"No reason why we can't go again, is there?"

"Jupiter's the best. It's *enormous*. A thousand times bigger than Earth, did you know that? You know what it looks like, Grandfather? Like my father's shooter. It's the same colors—

orange and brown and white, and sort of streaky, you know?"

"I've seen pictures of it, and it does indeed look like a marble."

"It has four big moons. Lots of other littler ones, too, but four with nice names only I can't remember them."

"Io, Ganymede, Europa, and Callisto," said Aunt Linzy. At Thomas's admiring look, she said, "Bookkeepers have good memories."

"How did you enjoy the voyage, Linzy?" Grandfather asked.

"Very much. But if it hadn't been for Thomas's baseball glove, I'd not have been able to see it at all. My neck, you know."

"No, I didn't know."

"Well, it's a pain in the neck, my neck," she said, with a little laugh. "But this dear boy lent me his glove for a pillow, and I was able to see the entire show."

"I always knew that glove would come in handy for something besides catching foul balls. May come in handy for that, too, one day," Grandfather added, forestalling Thomas. "Nothing's impossible."

Aunt Linzy didn't say, as she sometimes did, that everything was impossible.

They had a good dinner. For Grandfather and Thomas, grouper grilled in the backyard. For all three of them, black beans and rice, salad from the garden, mango ice cream from the freezer, and Grandfather's brownies.

Afterward there was a Cubs-Cardinals game, which Chicago, within two games of clinching the division, lost. Grandfather turned off the radio, telling Thomas not to worry—unless the Cubbies lost five straight, it was in the bag.

Aunt Linzy, who'd been doing the all-blue jigsaw for the second time, looked up and smiled at them. It occurred to Thomas that either Aunt Linzy was getting easier to have around or they were getting used to having her around. Which maybe came to the same thing, probably.

Later, lying in the dark, he tried to picture

Voyager II with its tiny twenty-two watt radio signal whispering messages to Earth from trillions of miles into space. He tried to force himself to understand how, when it got past Neptune, the little structure would journey on and on, into the starry reaches of forever. . . .

"Grandfather?"

"Thomas?"

"Are you asleep?

"No, no."

"Well—I was wondering . . . "

"Yes, Thomas? You were wondering. . . ?"

"Do you understand about space and about the universe never ending?"

"No."

"I can't make myself *feel* that space doesn't have any end, or that all those planets are going around out there in their orbits—and Voyager II going on and on in space without ever stopping. I mean, I guess I *believe* the universe is there and all that stuff's really going on, right *now* this minute, and all the time, because they say so, but it's awfully hard to understand. It's—mysterious."

"Thomas, I think even the people who *plot* the exploration of space would say they don't understand it."

"Then how do they do that? How do they decide what to do? How do they build things like Voyager II? Make them work, and make them take pictures, and change directions in space, and—all those other things they do? How *do* they?"

"All I can say, Thomas, is that the human species is capable of wonders. To me, the greatest wonder is that with all our marvelous capacity, our history is such a waste of war and hatred. Human beings, Thomas . . . we are far more impossible to comprehend than interstellar space."

"Sometimes I think I don't understand *anything*."

"Most of the time I know I don't."

"So—what are we going to do about it?"

"What we can, Thomas. What we can."

THE DAY THE PLAY-OFFS BEGAN, Aunt Linzy said she was going to town for paint, brushes, turpentine, and so forth.

"How much is it going to cost, including 'and so forth'?" Grandfather asked.

"How can I tell that beforehand, Joseph? I'll pay, and you can reimburse me. No charge for labor," she added, laughing.

"Linzy—it's a fine offer, no question of that, but are you sure you're up to doing this?"

"I am always sure of what I am up to doing. If not, I don't say I'm going to do it."

"Well. Well, well. Thomas and I plan to assist,

122

of course, when we have time—"

"That's all right, Joseph. If you can, fine. If not, that's fine, too. Now, I've been thinking that instead of this drab exterior gray—maybe it was white to begin with—"

"It's always been gray."

"Yes. I shan't ask when it was last painted. But what about a real change? Wouldn't barn red be a pickup? What do you say?"

"Sounds sort of violent." Grandfather looked at Thomas. "What do you say?"

"I think it sounds *great*," said Thomas, feeling a stir of interest in the project. "I'll help, Aunt Linzy. I mean, when there isn't any—"

"Yes, yes. When you aren't fishing and there's no baseball to attend to. I'll just get the truck keys, then." She turned at the kitchen door and said, "Still—there's no game until this afternoon, is there, Thomas?"

"Nope. American League game starts at three, if I can stand to listen. Tonight there's the Cubs and Giants, of course. I could come with you now, if you want."

"Just what I had in mind. We can select a

good red together, and a nice off-white for the trim, wouldn't you say?"

"Sure thing," said Thomas.

They went first to a paint store for everything Aunt Linzy said they'd need, then to a cafeteria for lunch. As Thomas hardly ever had a meal out, choosing what to put on his tray was a problem.

"How can anyone decide in time?" he asked his aunt, when he'd got past the section loaded with good desserts and arrived at just fruit but couldn't go back because of the people shoving behind him. "I wanted one of those peach pies or maybe the chocolate cake, only we get pushed *along* so fast—"

"Which do you want?" Aunt Linzy asked.

"Well, the cake, I guess, but you can't—"

"Watch my tray," she said, and stepped back along the line, reached through for a plate of heavily iced chocolate cake, and returned to Thomas without appearing to notice irritable glances sent her way. "Have to stick up for yourself," she said. Thomas regarded her admiringly.

When they got home, he didn't bother with the game. It was more fun fussing around with his great-aunt as she prepared her materials for house painting.

Post-season play got off to a terrible start, so far as Thomas and Grandfather were concerned, and from there on got worse. To begin with, the Cubs lost to the San Francisco Giants.

"Puts me in mind," said Grandfather, "of Jack and the Beanstalk, except that when the Cubbies got to the top, they found not one Giant, but a whole line-up of heavy bats."

They switched allegiance to the Giants, who lost the first two games in Oakland. During the first game in San Francisco there was an earthquake. Although the Series was resumed in a few days, Oakland taking it in four straight, Grandfather and Thomas didn't listen.

On the first Thursday of November, Milo McCallam arrived for a long weekend, bringing rods, reel, creel, lures, waders, and a wheel of Wisconsin cheddar for a house present.

Grandfather and Thomas were in back, in

the garden, planting bok choy and carrots, when they heard the car pull into the front drive, and then a shout of annoyance.

"I guess Ivan's offering his customary welcome," said Grandfather. "We'd better get out there and fend him off."

At the front of the house, they found Ivan nibbling gently on Mr. McCallam's shoe and Aunt Linzy explaining that he was a misunderstood duck who only needed affection and understanding to become a first-rate pet.

Mr. McCallam and Grandfather pounded each other on the back.

"Milo—good to have you," Grandfather exclaimed. "Linzy, this is our friend, Milo McCa—"

"We've introduced each other," Mr. McCallam said. "She's unfolding the inner Ivan to me. I reserve judgment, but there seems a slight improvement since the last time he attacked me. Not in looks, I regret to say." He handed the cheese to Grandfather. "Something for the larder, Joseph. How about a nice cold drink, eh? I've had a long drive across awful Alligator Alley."

"Linzy makes superior lemonade, if that appeals."

"Splendid! That is—if it's not too much—"

"Certainly not! It would be my *pleasure!*"

She almost ran up the steps, followed by Ringo.

Mr. McCallam stared at the house, scratching his head as if perplexed. "What's *happened* here, Joseph?"

"Huh?"

"Well—I can see you got the place painted at last, but how come? You've always liked the weather-beaten neglected look."

"Very funny. Are you coming in or aren't you?"

"A moment more, Joseph, to admire this transformation. Barn red! I'm impressed."

"Humph," muttered Grandfather. He didn't like the new color, but Thomas thought it looked fine.

They went inside, and again Mr. McCallam

stopped as if dumbfounded. Striking his forehead, he exclaimed, "I can't drink in all these marvels! Slipcovers on the furniture! Curtains at the windows! That delicate layer of dust and sand quite gone! And the windows! Someone has *washed* them! Joseph, your cottage has become your castle!"

"You go too far, Milo."

"Who is responsible for this transformation?"

"Ringo did it with his little cat's paw."

"Thomas . . . you'll make me a sensible answer. Is your aunt the magician here? She got your grandfather to finally hire painters and so forth?"

"She did it all her own self, Mr. McCallam. Painted the outside, and made the curtains and the—all the rest of it. It's so clean in here because she's always scrubbing things. Grandfather calls her the cleanup hitter."

"She painted the whole house? By *herself*?"

"We helped. Some."

"Well! You two really landed in hog heaven, didn't you, Joseph."

"If you want to put it that way," Grandfather said, and added, "I wouldn't."

While Aunt Linzy was in the kitchen, Grandfather said, "Look, Milo . . . there's a bit of difficulty about the sleeping arrangements—"

"I can see where there would be. Maybe I shouldn't've come."

Grandfather frowned. "If Thomas and I can rearrange our ways practically permanently, you can tolerate me as a roommate for a weekend. You take the bed, I'll use the cot."

"Oh, no, no—"

"Oh, yes, yes. Don't argue. Thomas on the living-room couch, you and me together in my room, you in the bed. That's it."

"You say it's a permanent arrangement? With, uh—" Milo tipped his head toward the kitchen.

"I—we—don't know. We take things day by day."

"How wise. It's the only way, the only way."

When Aunt Linzy came in with the tray, Mr. McCallam got up and took it from her. While the three settled for a talk, Thomas gulped his lemonade and said he'd finish the planting. Ringo followed, and they stayed in the garden, Ivan patrolling outside the fence, until Aunt Linzy called from the back porch for Thomas to come get the basket and collect salad things.

"What time are we going out in the morning?" Mr. McCallam asked at dinner.

"High tide's at six thirty-eight. To catch the incoming, we'll have to be out by six at the latest."

"The boat or the dock?"

"We thought tomorrow Thomas and I would fish from the dock. You can join us or use your waders. Saturday we'll take the boat, and then decide on Sunday which to do. That suit?"

"Fine, just fine," said Mr. McCallam. He smiled at the prospect of the weekend, then sighed heavily. "I hate to bring this up, but might as well get it said and over with. The thing is—this will probably be my last trip here for a long time."

"*Why?*" Thomas almost shouted. He looked

forward to these visits when he, Grandfather, and Mr. McCallam fished and cooked and played games in the evening and talked . . . and just were *together.*

He was used to these times, and did not want them to end.

Was Mr. McCallam annoyed because things had changed so much? Because he was obliged to sleep in the same room with Grandfather? Maybe he didn't like Aunt Linzy . . . except he seemed to. They'd spent over an hour in the afternoon working on the jigsaw puzzle with colored swirls. They'd talked about all sorts of stuff. Mr. McCallam told what running a motel was like, and Aunt Linzy talked about how she'd enjoyed her bookkeeping job for so many years. She said she preferred Florida to Chicago, and Mr. McCallam said, "Good, good." They agreed about not liking baseball much. "I'm into football and basketball," Mr. McCallam said, "but not in over my head." He'd looked over at Thomas and Grandfather and smiled to show he was kidding . . . sort of. They'd also discussed politics and seemed to agree on that, too. Grandfather said it was important for people to know right away where they stood on politics. That way unpleasant surprises didn't crop up later on in a friendship.

So if all of that was all right, why was this going to be Mr. McCallam's last visit?

He looked across the table and said, "I don't understand. *Why* is this maybe gonna be your last—"

He stopped, unable to go on.

Mr. McCallam reached over and patted his hand. "Possibly I overstate the situation, Thomas. I may be able to work things out. But Chet—that's my nephew, Linzy, who guards the gate when I'm away—has got what he's always wanted, a permanent appointment as a ranger out in Glacier Park. He'll be leaving as soon as I get back. I'm happy for him, of course, but it leaves me in a fix. Until now, I could always hand things over to Chet and leave without a qualm. But now—well, it's going to be a problem."

"Chet can't be the only reliable person you

know," Grandfather said. "Put your mind to it and find someone."

"I'm going to try, Joseph. But intelligent, trustworthy people don't grow on trees."

"Don't look in trees. Advertise. Interview people. There must be a way."

"Stop growling at me. I don't like it any better than you do. But you never ran a business, did you?"

"You know darn well I didn't," said Grandfather, who'd been a mailman all his working life.

"So you don't know what you're talking about. Well, it's my problem; I'll have to deal with it. How's for that cribbage game?"

It was Grandfather and Thomas's turn to do the dishes. They went to the kitchen while Mr. McCallam and Aunt Linzy finished, apparently without difficulty, the swirly jigsaw.

"It's funny, Grandfather, how she can do those like a snap, and we can hardly get started on them. And now Mr. McCallam, too. I mean, he's better at them than we are."

"Each to his specialty, Thomas. You and I double-skunked them at cribbage."

"Grandfather?"

"Thomas?"

"Don't you think—I mean, won't Mr. Mc-Callam—do you think he *really* won't come back again, on account of Chet, and nobody else being reliable?"

Grandfather sighed. "I don't know. Everything's changing, and I don't like it."

"Me, either. I don't like it at all."

Suddenly Grandfather laughed. "Come now, Thomas. It's all right for a grandparent to grumble about change, but not someone your age. Do you want to be a ten-year-old fogey?"

"I want things to be the way they were before—I mean, the way they once were."

"Well, that's then, this is now, and there's one sure thing in life, Thomas. You can't go back in time, no matter how much you want to. Besides, it's really not as bad as all that, is it? In some ways, I find your aunt likable, even if she does use scouring powder on everything but Ringo and Ivan."

Thomas's mouth twitched. Grandfather could always make him smile.

"She's okay," he said, adding, "in some ways."

"Of course she is."

Grandfather put the dishes away while Thomas, to save time in the morning, set the table for breakfast. Actually they'd eat almost nothing before setting off to start the weekend's fishing.

Thomas could hardly wait, and didn't mind when the mantel clock struck nine and Grandfather yawned and said they'd better get started for bed so as to catch the morning tide.

"How about you, Linzy?" Mr. McCallam asked. "Are you a fisherperson, like the rest of us?"

Thomas stiffened, prepared to hear how wicked it was to catch poor defenseless fish. Aunt Linzy only said no, she didn't care for the "sport." She did sort of bear down on the word "sport."

Grandfather's right, Thomas thought, lying on the living-room sofa for the first time in months. That was then and this is now, there's no way to go back, and maybe it's not so awful.

In some ways, Aunt Linzy had made things nicer. Thomas missed his room, and he didn't enjoy being straightened up after all the time. But he liked the curtains at the windows and the matching slipcovers. He liked the new color of the house even if Grandfather didn't. He'd had fun that day at the planetarium, and the other time in the cafeteria.

Ringo raced into the living room, leaped to the sofa, and settled down, asking to have his stomach stroked. It was Ringo, Thomas supposed, who mostly made him feel that having Aunt Linzy live with them wasn't so bad and in some ways was maybe pretty good.

Because Ringo—after having what Grandfather called a flirtation—had remembered that he was Thomas's cat. He paid attention to Aunt Linzy but waited once more for Thomas to come home from school, followed him to the garden, got on his lap when they were playing games, and except for every once in a while, slept where Thomas slept. It was like the old days. And wasn't that, in a way, going back in time?

Thomas's eyes closed, his hand fell away from the cat's sturdy, sleek-furred body, and they were asleep.

9

M R. MCCALLAM, IN HIS WADERS, cast from
the low surf. Thomas and Grandfather were
fishing as usual from an old dock that jutted
into the Gulf of Mexico. Beneath it, stretching
to either side, was what remained of a seawall.
It had been built to hold the ocean back from a
house that a hurricane had long ago swept out
to sea, leaving the seawall and the dock behind. At low tide marine cockroaches, crabs,
and other sea creatures crawled over and under the barnacled rocks that had formed the
wall. Now the water covered them and was rising under the dock.

As Grandfather dropped his cast net over a

school of glass minnows, getting enough for the morning's bait, a great blue heron sailed to a feet-first stop at the end of the dock, folded its wings, and began a stately, self-assured march toward the bait bucket. It was allowed to help itself to three or four minnows before Grandfather put the lid on, indicating that breakfast was over for now.

"Later," he said to the heron. "If we fare well, you will, too. Hang around."

No need to tell the heron to hang around. No need to inform a flotilla of pelicans, rising and falling gently on the waves a few feet from Mr. McCallam, that they, too, would benefit from patience.

Grandfather sometimes said that human beings would do well to study the animal world and learn the rewards of patience and self-command. Thomas, a restless boy, sometimes watched Ringo sit unmoving at a hole in the ground for what seemed hours. He'd decide to try being patient and self-commanding, setting himself a goal of not moving for ten minutes at least. But, as he explained to Donny, he was too jumpy to keep it up, and had never got to *two* minutes.

"You know something, Grandfather?" Thomas said, moving his rod in small, gentle jerks.

"I daresay I do."

"No! I mean, did you notice something?"

"Much has come to my notice."

"Grandfather, you're teasing."

"Sorry. What should I have noticed?"

"That she doesn't tell Mr. McCallam how mean and horrible it is to fish. Why's that?"

"Because he's a guest, I suppose. It would be impolite to say to a guest that he's going to do something mean and horrible."

"So why isn't it impolite to tell us we are?"

"For some reason, Thomas, what's rudeness to a stranger is considered candor with relatives. Don't ask me why."

"Why can't I ask you why?"

"Because I don't have an answer. You'd think we'd be even politer to friends and relations than to folks we don't know, but it hardly ever works out that way."

140

"Did you hear when he asked if she liked football she said she'd never tried but it might be of interest?"

"Did she, now? I missed that."

"She said it when they were doing the jigsaw together."

"Humph," said Grandfather. "Fancy that. Perhaps the wind sits in a direction we've not noticed. Thomas, hush! I've got a nibble."

The fishing was bountiful on Friday and Saturday, the meals tasty, the evenings—spent playing cards or cribbage, or in conversation—a success.

But the big news, the important event, came Sunday afternoon. It was a surprise that Grandfather later said should not have taken them by surprise, all things considered, but nevertheless it had.

"Probably," Thomas said, "because we didn't consider all things."

"The signs were there," Grandfather said. "Practically billboards. It comes of not looking at billboards. Of not testing the wind direction."

Grandfather, Mr. McCallam, and Thomas had spent Sunday morning cruising in the boat, throwing back all but one big redfish that Thomas hooked.

"I've no complaints," Mr. McCallam said. He was going to take a good part of his weekend catch back to Miami.

After lunch, when Aunt Linzy left to take her turn in the kitchen, Mr. McCallam said, "Joseph. Thomas. Please sit. I have something to say."

He looked stern and serious.

Grandfather and Thomas exchanged glances, took their chairs, and sat quiet as in a courtroom.

"You are both aware of my dilemma with the motel, with Chet's leaving and all."

"I don't know what the 'and all' is," said Grandfather, "but yes, we are aware of your dilemma. You've mentioned it several times since you arrived."

"You're getting crotchety, Joseph. A good friend should warn you about that."

"A good friend frequently does warn me."

"It's meant for your own good."

"I'm sure you mean it so. You have a point to make, Milo?"

"Yes, of course. Yes, I have. Now . . . Linzy and I have had occasion to—to talk with each other this weekend. We get along well together. Agree on many things. Politics, football, interior decor . . . "

Grandfather lifted one eyebrow.

"Well, not to make too long a palaver, I've offered her a job."

"Job?" said Grandfather. "Aha! At the motel, right?"

"Right. You know, she really is an amazing person. Stable and sensible and kindly. Look how nice she is to that ill-humored duck. I mean, the woman has a good heart, and good taste, besides being an excellent housekeeper, and on top of all that, she's a bookkeeper. I hate keeping books."

"What's she supposed to do in this job? I feel some responsibility, after all. She's Marta's sister."

"Don't fret, Joseph. I'm making her my

manager, in place of Chet. Good pay, her own quarters. I can't tell you, Joseph—and Thomas—how pleased I am. This means, you understand, that I can continue to come over here, and our times together will go on uninterrupted."

"It means more than that," said Grandfather. "Not that we aren't pleased to know you'll be coming as usual—" He broke off and pinched the end of his nose. He's thinking, Thomas said to himself, and waited for the result.

"Milo," Grandfather said at last, "this sounds fine for you, but are you sure it's what Linzy herself wants?"

"Yes, Joseph," said Aunt Linzy at the living-room door. "It is the sort of chance I've dreamed of. I am grateful to you, and to Thomas, for putting up with me all this—"

"Linzy! We didn't put *up* with—"

"Yes." She came in and sat in her favorite chair. Ringo jumped to her lap and she stroked him absently. "It's got better as time passed, and I flatter myself that I've made some contribution to your well-being—not that you wanted everything I contributed, but nevertheless—"

"Linzy—"

"Neverthe*less*, I think I leave you in better shape than I found you."

"We don't question that—"

Aunt Linzy held up her hand. "No need to protest, Joseph. I am aware of sacrifices made on my behalf." She looked at Thomas. "Did I ever thank you properly—or at all—for letting me have your room?"

Thomas wriggled and screwed up his face. "Sure."

"No. I fear not. You were most kind, most kind." She ran her hand down Ringo's back, looked on him fondly, bent an equally fond eye on Thomas. "You're a good boy. You share, and you don't complain about it."

Thomas didn't know what to say, but Grandfather rescued him. "Linzy, are you certain you want to work for this fellow?" He waved a hand at Mr. McCallam. "I expect he can be a demanding taskmaster."

"Oh, that'll be all right. Just so I have a job. I miss working."

"Miss it? You're always doing something. I never see you at rest."

"I miss having a *job*. Something I have to do, and that I get paid for. I can't understand how you enjoy retirement the way you seem to, Joseph."

"To each his own," said Grandfather. "I dote on being retired."

"As you say, to each his own. Well. I shall get my things in order and rent a U-Haul for next weekend. Milo is sending a man up to drive back with me. There's only—"

She hesitated, looking from Thomas to Grandfather.

"Yes, Linzy?" Grandfather prodded.

"Well—it's the animals. I think they'd miss me—"

Thomas's mouth dropped open, but before he could speak, Grandfather, quirking an eyebrow, said, "What are you getting at, Linzy?"

"I only wondered if maybe—" She looked at the cat in her lap, then at Thomas. "No, of course not. But perhaps you'd let Ivan come with me? Milo says there's no reason why he shouldn't patrol the motel grounds, as long as he stays a bachelor. Which, so far, he has."

"My dear Linzy—you are *welcome* to Ivan. I'm positive he'd pine away to nothing but a bone and a feather without you, and we certainly don't want that." He looked at Mr. McCallam. "You know his disposition, Milo. You're prepared?"

"I'm prepared to endure, since it's what Linzy wants."

"Well," said Grandfather. "Well, well . . . what a turn of events! It calls for a celebration. Let's have some of Linzy's excellent lemonade and some of my equally excellent chocolate cake!"

After Mr. McCallam had driven off, and Aunt Linzy had gone to her room (my room soon, thought Thomas; my room again) to start sorting and packing, Thomas and Grandfather sat on the front-porch swing, Ringo on the railing. A clear, tomato-colored sunset, banded with green, spread over the Gulf of Mexico, as darkness gathered in the garden. The evening insect chorus rose from the earth, and from shadowed branches came the occasional chirrup of a nesting bird. A crow landed in the birdbath, splashed happily for a moment, and flew off. A barred owl barked.

Thomas said, "She was going to ask could she take Ringo, too, wasn't she?"

"We can't be sure of that."

"I'm sure."

"She reconsidered in time."

"Yeah. Grandfather?"

"Thomas?"

"Remember that time she dropped the dish of spaghetti on the floor, because a cockroach ran in front of her?"

Grandfather nodded, smiling. "How about the day I caught her just as she was about to wash my pipes? That was a close thing."

"And she was always trying to help me with things I don't want to be helped with. Like arithmetic."

"I suppose," said Grandfather, "we'll do this from time to time. Remember different things about your aunt's visit. Some good things, too, right?"

"I guess. I mean, I liked it when she took me to the planetarium. And how she worked so hard painting the house. Times like that we'll remember."

The swing creaked as they idly pushed it back and forth. "This's cozy, isn't it, Grandfather?"

"Cozy's the word."

"Funny," Thomas said. "Now I don't really remember much bad about it. The visit. Except not having my room, except I kind of like being in with you. And Ringo likes me again." He stopped, frowning. "Isn't that funny, Grandfather? I mean, how it's hard to remember anything awful, when we—I—was so upset, in the beginning?"

"I can't think how or why, considering the trouble and pain there is in life, we mostly tend to remember the good parts and put the bad out of mind."

"That's lucky, isn't it?"

"It certainly is."

Aunt Linzy turned on the living-room lamps

and a yellow square of light fell over the porch, across the hibiscus bush. In a moment the screen door creaked as she came out to sit in her rocker.

"Have you been to Milo's motel?" she asked. "Either of you?"

"Just me," said Grandfather. "You'll like it. Very clean and pretty. Lots of flowers. Air-conditioning."

"Perhaps you'll come to see me sometime, with Thomas?"

"I don't see why not."

They creaked and rocked, not speaking, for a while.

Then, "Oh, my," said Aunt Linzy. "It's so lovely here in the evening. I shall miss it."

"We'll miss you, too," Grandfather said.

"That's as may be. No, no—don't protest, Joseph. I am aware of the drawbacks we've all felt. On the other hand, I feel sure that you're sincere enough so that when I say I'd like to visit you again someday, you won't say no."

"We *want* you to visit us, Aunt Linzy," Thomas said.

He had looked up the word "visit" in their dictionary. It had a lot of definitions, but the one that leaped off the page at him was: "to call upon or sojourn with friends for a short time."

So. He would like to have her visit them. Sojourn with them. Sometime. For a short time.

Later, in their room, getting ready for bed, Thomas said, "Grandfather, if Bobby Bo does get traded to some other team, what do we do then?"

"Go on rooting for Pittsburgh, of course. They'll still be a good team, believe me."

"It won't be the same. It won't be like it was before."

"Life, Thomas. Life, going its way, changing us and everything around us. I admit that rosters in the majors seem to change faster than light. Used to be a man stayed with one team for his whole career, but those days are gone."

Thomas frowned. "Just the same," he said, almost combatively, "it's still a—the most wonderful game of all."

"Of course it is. Magic, wherever it's played. Sandlots, the minors, the majors. If it's baseball, it's magic."

For a while Grandfather read and Thomas lay thinking, one hand on the sleeping Ringo.

"Grandfather?" he said at last.

"Thomas?"

"Would you tell me something?"

"If I can."

"She—Aunt Linzy—she's glad to be going to Mr. McCallam's motel?"

"Very much so, I'd say."

"So if she is, then it's all right for me to be glad she's leaving here?"

"All right, and perfectly normal."

"Well, that's okay, then."

Grandfather yawned and turned out the light.

"Good night, Thomas," said Grandfather. "Pleasant dreams."

"Good night, Grandfather. See you in the morning."

Ringo leaped to Thomas's bed. Hands beneath his head, Thomas looked at the outline of his Bobby Bonilla baseball on the windowsill. Outside, palm fronds rustled with a sound like rain, and from somewhere in the dark came the fluttering call of a screech owl. Some things, thought Thomas, do stay the same.

Waiting for sleep, Thomas thought about spring training, the only time when he and Grandfather got to go to real games, played in the afternoon, in the sun, on grass. He heard the thud of the ball as it hit the glove, saw fielders go into their crouch, watched them leap, dive, whirl to throw for a double play. He watched the windup, the delivery, the catch, the scoop at first, saw the ball rise and rise through the mild blue air and disappear from the ball park as a player circled the bases in his home-run trot. And, clear as clear, he heard the roar of utter joy from the stands as an impossible catch somehow, miraculously, magically, anyway got caught. . . .

AUTHOR'S NOTE

This book was conceived and written during the summer of '89, when Bobby Bonilla *still* played for the Pittsburgh Pirates.

Mary Stolz